DON'T
CALL ME
ISHMAEL

DON'T CALL ME ISHMAEL

MICHAEL GERARD BAUER

templar

A TEMPLAR BOOK

First published by Omnibus Books,

an imprint of Scholastic Australia Pty Ltd, 2006

Published in the UK in 2012 by Templar Publishing,

an imprint of The Templar Company Limited,

The Granary, North Street, Dorking, Surrey,

RH4 1DN, UK

www.templarco.co.uk

Cover designed by crushed.co.uk

First UK edition

Mixed Sources
Product group from well-managed
forests and other controlled sources
www.fsc.org Cert no. SA-COC-1565
© 1996 Forest Stewardship Council
FSC

ISBN 978-1-84877-683-8

Printed and bound by CPI Group (UK) Ltd,

Croydon, CR0 4YY

To Greg, Keith and Anne,
because it's all about friendship, love and laughter...
and because I took your threats seriously.

CONTENTS

Part 1

Part 2

Part 3

Part 4

Part 5

Part 1

Call me Ishmael.

HERMAN MELVILLE, *Moby Dick*

1.
The Mayor of Loserville

There's no easy way to put this, so I'll just say it straight out. It's time I faced up to the truth. I'm fourteen years old and I have Ishmael Leseur's Syndrome.

There is no cure.

Now, as far as I know, I'm the only recorded case of Ishmael Leseur's Syndrome in the world. In fact, the medical profession has probably never even heard of Ishmael Leseur's Syndrome. But it's real, believe me. The problem is, though, who *would* believe me?

For a while there I guess I was in denial, but this year the symptoms have been just too painful and horrifying to ignore. And I'm not exaggerating here. No way. I'm telling you, Ishmael Leseur's Syndrome is capable of turning an otherwise almost normal person into a walking disaster registering nine point nine on the open-ended imbecile scale.

That's why I have decided to write all this down. Now everyone will finally understand the truth, and instead of electing me the Mayor of Loserville, they'll simply shake their heads, smile kindly and say, "It's all right. We understand. The poor boy has Ishmael Leseur's Syndrome. It's not his fault."

Anyway, maybe I'm getting ahead of myself here. I should really start at the beginning and go through things thoroughly – after all, I guess this needs to be approached scientifically if I'm to convince you that what I claim is true.

So, first things first. My name is Ishmael Leseur.

Now wait a moment, I know what you're going to say – I have the same name as my condition! You probably think I just invented it so I can use it as an excuse whenever I make a complete fool of myself. But you don't get it. It's not that simple. You have to understand that the name is the condition – or at least part of it. I'm not absolutely sure of the precise details of how it works. After all, I'm not a scientist, I'm just the victim here, but I do have my theories, and this is one of them.

> THEORY ONE: Ishmael Leseur's Syndrome is triggered by the release of a deadly virus that results from the combination of the words 'Ishmael' and 'Leseur'.

Now, I have thought about this a lot, so let me explain some of my conclusions. As I see it, the individual letters by themselves are harmless. The combination of letters forming the separate words 'Ishmael' and 'Leseur' also seem relatively harmless. To illustrate this I refer to the other members of my immediate family: namely, my father Ron Leseur, insurance salesman and co-founder of the 1980's rock group the Dugongs, my mother Carol Leseur, local councillor and chief family organiser, and my thirteen year-old sister Prue Leseur.

Now, as you can see, each of the above carries the name Leseur, yet I assure you that none of them suffers from any of the horrible symptoms that you are about to hear described. In fact, I'd have to say that most of the time my mother and father seem painfully happy and content and, to rub it in, my sister Prue, according to every friend, relative and stranger who has ever set eyes on her, is 'adorable'. She also has an IQ somewhere near genius level. In fact, if brains were cars, Prue would be a Rolls Royce while I would be a Goggomobil up on blocks with half its engine missing. And how do you think that makes me feel? Well, I'll tell you. Like the only person ever rejected for the job of village idiot because he was *waaaay* overqualified. Or, as Prue so thoughtfully explained it to me one day, "Human beings use only ten per cent of their brain, which would seem, in your case, Ishy, nowhere near enough."

So there you have it. The only conclusion you can possibly draw from my family's immunity to the syndrome is that it is triggered only by the fatal combination of the words 'Ishmael' and 'Leseur'.

The way *I* see it is, the linking of these particular sounds must result in some kind of chemical reaction that germinates a virus, which then mutates the cells of the body, causing an increase in deadly toxins.

These deadly toxins then infect the brain and nervous system, which results in the sufferer saying and doing things that would embarrass even a complete moron. I haven't quite been able to prove this theory yet: science is not my best subject. I'm much better at English, actually, but who wouldn't be with Miss Tarango as your teacher? But that's another story, and as Miss often reminds me, I have to watch my 'structuring' when I write. Apparently I have a tendency to wander off the point.

Anyway, the point is, I didn't end up with Ishmael Leseur's Syndrome because of any chance combining of those two words. Oh no. I am who I am because of a deliberate act. You see, I know the circumstances surrounding the creation of my name in excruciating detail, and I know exactly who is responsible.

I will record their names now in this diary for all to see.

The ones who burdened me with the curse of Ishmael Leseur's were my parents. That's right, the afore-mentioned (this is an excellent word in a serious document such as this – Miss Tarango would approve) Ron and Carol Leseur. You can't blame them, of course.

Parents are supposed to name their children. What happened wasn't their fault. They had no idea what a terrible thing they were doing.

Perhaps, though, I would find it a little easier to accept if they hadn't been laughing hysterically at the time they did it.

2.
FANCY THAT

The story of how I got my name is a family favourite. Well, at least it's my *father's* favourite. Each member of the family has a slightly different reaction to it. Dad just loves to tell it. Mum just loves to hear it. Prue just loves to watch me squirm when it's told. And me? I just squirm.

I have heard the how-Ishmael-got-the-name-Ishmael story so many times I feel as if I was there myself. And of course, in a way I was. It's just that most of the time I was floating like a chubby alien in a sea of amniotic fluid, blissfully unaware that there were people outside the cosy warmth of my mother's womb who were about to change my life forever.

Now it's a known fact that no one and nothing can stop my father telling the how-Ishmael-got-the-name-Ishmael story when he's made up his mind to. And it doesn't matter if the intended audience has heard it all before or not. Oh no. I couldn't begin to count the number of times I've heard something like the following exchange:

Dad: Did I ever tell you the story of how Ishmael got his name?

Victim: Yes. Yes, I think you did. Wasn't your wife in hospital… and she was overdue…

Dad: That's right, she was way overdue. I'll never forget it. It's a great story. I came to visit her after work…

Victim: Yes. I remember. You told me. A great story – how your wife was feeling a bit upset and said she felt like a…

Dad: Upset! I'll say. You should have been there. When I came to visit her after work she'd been crying…

Victim: Yeah, yeah, and she said she was so big she felt like a…

Dad: She was huge! And you know it was our first
           baby and, being overdue, she was tired and
           worried, so it was pretty hard for her.
           Anyway, as I was saying, when I came to visit
           after work…

Around about this point Dad's victims usually realise
that resistance is useless. Their faces become set with
a weak smile that from time to time is accompanied by
a shake of the head and a raising of the eyebrows to
signal that they are suitably amazed and impressed in
the appropriate places. Rarely do they attempt to
interrupt, and then it is only to offer such morsels as,
'Really?', 'Fancy that' or 'You don't say'. And meanwhile
Dad rumbles on like a runaway steam train that can't
be stopped until it has found its final resting place in
some unsuspecting lounge room.

My dad might appear harmless enough, but the
'Ishmael' tale is always there, lurking just below the
surface of every conversation, like some massive
crocodile with only its eyes breaking the water, poised
and ready to strike. And all it takes is for some unsuspecting victim to step too close to the water's edge.

"Ishmael? That's an interesting name."

And they're gone. Any thought of rescue is pointless. My father will have already exploded from the shallow water of idle chit-chat, seized his bewildered prey and dragged it thrashing into the shadowy depths of his memories.

This leads me to another of my theories.

THEORY TWO: The carrier of Ishmael Leseur's Syndrome can trigger disturbing behaviour in others.

At first I thought this phenomenon was isolated to my father, but that was before I encountered Barry Bagsley. I realised then that my father's symptoms were actually mild and that the name Ishmael Leseur could bring out the very worst in people. Barry Bagsley, however, will have to wait. It's time for a family favourite. Did I ever tell you the story of how I got my name?

3.
THAR SHE BLOWS!

According to the doctor, I was due before the end of July. By August the first, Mum had been in hospital for a week and after a number of false alarms had become, well, a little emotional.

"I feel like a whale!" she moaned repeatedly, holding on to her swollen stomach with both hands as if to stop it from exploding. Dad reckons that with her belly button popping out, it looked like she was being attacked by a giant breast. Apparently Mum failed to see the humour in this observation at the time and threw a bedpan at him. Like I said, she was a little emotional. Anyway, Dad decided that Mum needed cheering up. Or as he likes to put it, "I had to do something to stop her *whaling*."

But what happened next was no joke for me. Dad made an excuse to go outside, saying he was going to ring family and friends to give them a progress report. 20 minutes later he returned. But when she looked to where he was standing in the doorway, Mum found herself confronted by a cross between an escapee from a lunatic asylum and some kind of deranged pirate.

It seems that while Dad was away he had somehow convinced the nurses to help him strap his right leg up behind his thigh and to attach a hollow cardboard cylinder to his knee like a wooden stump. They also supplied him with an old wooden crutch, a surgical eye patch that they had coloured with a black marker and a bandanna made of gauze from which a tangle of Dad's red locks sprouted like mad snakes. The costume was topped off by a little blue teddy bear that was sticky-taped to my father's shoulder as a stand-in parrot.

Dad posed dramatically in the doorway, with his left hand thrust on his hip while he swayed unsteadily. "Arrrrr," he cried insanely, with eyes glinting at Mum's huge, pale belly, "I be Cap'n Ahab and I be seeking the white whale!"

Now that might have been the end of Dad's demented send-up if it hadn't been for the fact that Mum had just guzzled a mouthful of water and had been caught pre-swallow. Apparently, as Dad tells it, there was a second or two while my mother stared at him with her cheeks bulging like an 'obese goldfish' before a strange, gurgling, humming noise started in her mouth. Soon after, her belly began to shake like blancmange and her eyeballs, under the strain of jamming her mouth shut, looked as if they had decided it was time to abandon their sockets and leave home.

Eventually the pressure was just too much. Suddenly a short, sharp jet of water shot out from my mother's pursed lips, cleared the bulge of her stomach and scored a bullseye on the chart that hung from the end of her bed.

Dad's eyes widened with delight before he shouted triumphantly, "Arrrrr-arrrrrhhh! Thar she blows!"

And blow she did.

Dad describes the gush of water that came from Mum's mouth as 'Niagara Falls on a good day'. In between spluttering, choking and gasping for air, Mum laughed so hard that her own waters broke.

Then the contractions started and accelerated straight into overdrive.

When Dad realised that Mum was roaring as much with pain as with laughter, he sprang into action. Thrusting aside his crutch, he stepped boldly into the room. Unfortunately he had forgotten entirely about his 'wooden' leg. As the cardboard cylinder crumbled beneath Dad's weight, he lurched forward and made a desperate grab for the curtain that hung bunched at the end of the bed. A shower of curtain rings exploded into the air, ricocheted off the walls and ceiling and clattered around the room like plastic hail. At this point tears of laughter were rolling down my mother's face as she clutched her belly and shrieked hysterically, "No, please, stop it! Stop it! Oh please! No more, I can't bear it! Stop!"

Dad reckons he knew just how Mum felt at the time. With his leg strapped behind him when he fell, his knee had crashed helplessly into the hard linoleum floor and he was now on his back rocking in agony and choking with laughter. It didn't last long. A new sound began to fill the room. It was a deep, growling, grinding moan.

And then... well, I guess you know what happened next. Thankfully my parents have spared me the gruesome details. All I can say is that it wasn't long before Mum and Dad were gazing lovingly at their firstborn child. Me. We were one small happy family. Everything was perfect. Until…

"A boy, a beautiful boy," Mum said, wiping tears from her cheek. "But what about a name? We still haven't decided on a name."

Whenever Dad tells the next bit he does all the actions. The scene has become so familiar it's as if I remember it myself. He frowns, leans over with his ear hovering close to his newborn son's gurgling mouth and listens intently while his eyes dart back and forth as if he is hearing some wonderful secret.

"What's the little fella saying?" Mum asks.

Dad raises his head and looks at her in wonder. "He's saying… 'Call me Ishmael'!"

When the doctor finally bustled into Mum's room that fateful day around fourteen years ago, she found my parents dissolved in joyous, uncontrollable laughter with their baby son between them. I wasn't laughing though. Dad says I was "shrieking like a chainsaw".

Maybe even then I knew what my father had done to me.

4.
THANKS A LOT, HERMAN!

Of course there wouldn't even be any Ishmael Leseur's Syndrome if it weren't for Herman Melville. He's the real culprit.

That's right. The simple fact is, that if around one hundred and fifty years ago Herman Melville hadn't written his novel about Captain Ahab and his mad quest for the white whale *Moby Dick*, then Ron Leseur (my father) would never have studied it at university in American Literature A with Carol McCann (my mother). And if Herman Melville had never written Moby Dick and my parents hadn't studied it, then seven years later when they were married and expecting their first child (me), my father would never have dressed up as Captain Ahab just because my mother said she looked like a whale, since there wouldn't have been any Captain Ahab for him to dress up as, or any white whale for him to make a joke about, and therefore he would never have made Mum laugh so much that yours truly would be squeezed out screaming into the world before I was ready *and* (this is the *crucial* point) he would never have uttered the name Ishmael in a million years because he wouldn't have known that Ishmael was the name of the narrator and hero of the novel *Moby Dick* because Herman Melville would never have written it for my father to have read it and found that out and my mother wouldn't have laughed at it even if for some bizarre reason my father *had* mentioned the name Ishmael, because it wouldn't have made any sense to her any more seeing as how she wouldn't have read the book because there wouldn't have been any book to read since Melville wouldn't have written it. And if it hadn't been my terrible fate to end up as Ishmael Lescur then none of the disasters of my life would have happened and today I would be a happy normal teenager like everyone else my age.

It's as simple as that.

Now if you don't believe this is *all* true you can check for yourself. Go ahead, get a copy of *Moby Dick*. You don't even have to read every word. In fact you don't have to read very much at all – not even a chapter, not even a page. All you have to do is read three words. *Three words!* Go on. Turn to Chapter One. It's called 'Loomings'.

See, there it is on the very first page. Read the opening three words of *Moby Dick* by Herman Melville. They are the same words that my parents would have read at uni. The same words that were buried deep within my father's brain, lying there dormant until that awful day August the first, fourteen years ago, when they were germinated by the sight of my mother's swollen belly and watered by the tears of my parents' laughter.

Go on, read them. Read the first three words of *Moby Dick*. Here, I'll help you. *'Call me Ishmael.'*

Thanks a lot, Herman!

5.
A WUSSY-CRAP NAME

Now I don't want you to get the wrong idea. I haven't suffered from Ishmael Leseur's all my life. Far from it. In fact, for the first twelve years of my existence I showed no symptoms at all. Then I started secondary school at St Daniel's Boys College.

Before that I had spent seven uneventful years at Moorfield Primary among classmates who wouldn't have cared if my name were Slobo Bugslag (which, incidentally, was the name of the most popular kid in the school). However, things changed completely at the start of secondary school. With primary school over, our class moved on to a range of schools throughout town. Only a handful of us went to St Daniel's.

There my world changed dramatically. At Moorfield Primary I was in a class of twelve. On the first day at St Daniel's I stood in an assembly area with over a hundred new boys waiting to be divided into four classes. When I checked the class lists, I found I had been separated from the only two boys I knew from primary school. In our form room our teacher Mr Brownhill went through the roll to check that everyone was in the right place. Halfway through the list he said, 'Ishmael Leseur'.

I answered, "Here, sir," like everyone else before me.

"Ishmael?" he repeated, pausing for the first time during the register. "That's an interesting name."

Twenty-five sets of eyes turned to look at me. None of them seemed to find me the least bit interesting. One of those sets of eyes belonged to Barry Bagsley. Remember my second theory?

THEORY TWO: The carrier of Ishmael Leseur's Syndrome can trigger disturbing behaviour in others.

Well, Barry Bagsley was an extreme case in point.

I picked up the first subtle hint of this in his opening line to me in the playground that first day.

"Ishmael? What kind of a wussy-crap name is that?"

What could I say? Up to this point of my life I hadn't even known it was a wussy-crap name. No one had warned me that I had a wussy-crap name. Why would my parents give me a wussy-crap name in the first place? Was Herman Melville aware it was a wussy-crap name? All I could do was smile stupidly while Barry Bagsley and his friends laughed and pushed past me like I was a revolving door.

I stood there like a wuss.

I felt like crap.

That night I stared at myself in the bathroom mirror. Somehow I didn't look the same. It was like the time one of my friends said that he thought my left ear stuck out more than my right one. When I got home that day I measured them and they were exactly the same. But still every time I looked at my reflection I couldn't help thinking that one of my ears was giving a hand signal for a left turn. This felt the same. I was seeing myself in a different way. I looked different. But what could it be? Then it hit me.

I looked like a kid with a wussy-crap name. Not only that, I swear my left ear was jutting out like an open car door!

The next day when I walked into the classroom, Barry Bagsley was waiting.

"Hey, what stinks? Oh no! It's Fishtail Le Sewer!"

Yes, as I was saying, something about my name brought out the worst in Barry Bagsley. He ripped and tore at it like a mad dog mauling a shoe, until it became so mangled and twisted that even I had trouble remembering who I really was.

Ishmael was crunched into Fishtail. Fishtail was ground into Dishrail. Dishrail was mashed into Kisstail and Kisstail was slobbered into Piss-stale. And let's not forget all the various mutations and cross-pollinations like Fishstale, Stalefish, Stalepiss, Pisstrail, Email and Female.

Even my last name was not safe from mutilation. Leseur (actually pronounced Le-sir) became Le Sewer and then Le Spewer, Le Pooer and finally Manure. By the end of my first term of high school Barry Bagsley had miraculously transformed me from Ishmael Leseur to Stalepiss Manure.

And that summed up exactly how I felt.

6.

THE CREATURE FROM LE SEWER

It soon became obvious to every new boy that if you wanted to survive your stay at St Daniel's relatively unscathed, there were only two courses of action open to you: either avoid Barry Bagsley at all costs, which was what the majority chose to do, or risk the road less travelled and seek out the dangerous safety of Barry Bagsley's inner circle of 'friends'.

For me, avoidance was the only option.

I quickly realised that as long as I stayed as far away from Barry Bagsley as possible and didn't do anything stupid like, say, asking or answering a question in class, making some kind of unusual noise like shouting, laughing or speaking, volunteering for something, putting my name on a list, trying out for a sport, leaving an item of mine where it could be moved, thrown or written on, looking anywhere near the direction of Barry and his friends, or merely doing anything whatsoever that might indicate that I actually existed, then I would be fine.

Essentially, the most important lesson I learned last year was to make myself as small a target as possible. I became an expert at this. I became virtually invisible to Barry Bagsley and his mates. Sometimes I could barely see myself. So that was basically how I spent my first year at high school – in hiding. On the occasions when I was reluctantly flushed out into the open, like when I couldn't avoid answering a teacher's question, I prepared myself for the inevitable comments of, "What's that pong?" or "Who stepped in manure?" or "Oh my god! It's the creature from Le Sewer!" But even these insults lost a little sting eventually. After all, maybe they were right. Maybe I did stink. Isn't that what my name said?

Anyway, I somehow made it through to the end of the year, escaped gratefully into the Christmas holidays and returned reluctantly, fully expecting that school life for me would be much the same as before. I was wrong. This year would be different.

It would be the toughest, the weirdest, the most embarrassingly awful and the best year of my life.

7.
MOBY WHAT?

It was the first day back after the holidays. A brand new year. A brand new classroom. A brand new teacher leading our Tutor Group. A brand new start.

"Hey, Le Spewer – chuck us a red pen, will ya? You'd be good at *chuckin'*, wouldn't ya, Le *Spewer*?"

Same old Barry Bagsley. I mean, you certainly had to hand it to him. In his own way he really had quite a creative touch with language. Naturally, I gave as good as I got by pretending to be busy arranging my books and hoping like hell that our teacher would arrive soon. She did. Miss Tarango.

It would be pretty fair to say that none of us had

ever had a teacher like Miss Tarango before. She was young. She was beautiful. She actually seemed happy to be there. I think Mum would have described her as 'bubbly'. I liked her straight away. She had short curly blonde hair, eyes that actually did sparkle and dimples in her cheeks that appeared like magic whenever she smiled, which was often. She was also bright, friendly and enthusiastic. I couldn't see her surviving a term.

"Good morning, boys. My name is Miss Tarango. I'm your new English and Tutor Group teacher. This is my first year of teaching and *you* are my *very* first class."

Make that a week. Already I could hear rumblings from the back corner, where Barry and his mates were holed up like gangsters.

"All right, let's quieten down so I can take the register."

"I've registered her all right." Stifled laughter broke out from behind me.

Miss Tarango fixed her smiling face on Barry Bagsley. "I'm sorry, I missed that," she said pleasantly.

"Nothing, Miss," Barry Bagsley said with a smirk. "I was just saying that I was ready for the register."

The boys around him returned his smirk.

Miss Tarango held Barry Bagsley with her clear blue eyes and smiled. The rest of us waited. The rest of us waited some more. The rest of us wondered uneasily how much longer we were going to have to wait. The boys around Barry Bagsley lost their smirks. Miss Tarango remained silent and smiled like the cover shot of a glossy magazine. Barry Bagsley shifted a little in his seat.

"Well, thank you for your support. It's good to know we are of one mind. Now, let's get started, shall we? Let's see who we have here. Tom Appleby?"

"Here, Miss."

"Ryan Babic?"

"Here, Miss."

"Barry Bagsley?"

"Yo!"

Miss Tarango smiled pleasantly once more, but a little of the sparkle seemed missing from her eyes. "Barry, I think a simple 'Here' or 'Present' would be more appropriate and polite in future thank you."

The roll call continued again without incident until, "Ishmael... Now, is your surname pronounced Le-*sir*, Ishmael?"

"Yes, Miss."

"He's lying, Miss. It's Le-sewer. Fishtail Le-sewer!"

More laughter from behind me.

Miss Tarango placed the roll on the desk in front of her. She spoke calmly and deliberately. "Barry, I always try very hard to learn people's names and to pronounce them correctly. I expect the same from you and from everyone else in this class. Each one of us deserves to be treated with respect. I won't tolerate anything less. Please remember that in future. Okay?"

Barry Bagsley sat silently. Miss Tarango returned to her list of names.

"Where was I? Yes... Ishmael."

Then she stopped, looked up from the sheet and smiled at me. "You know, in fact Ishmael is quite a famous name in English literature."

What? Oh no. No, don't say it. Please don't say it. Just read the next name on the register. Just forget about it and go on. Please.

"Did you know that Ishmael was the name of the hero of a very famous novel?" Miss Tarango's face beamed enthusiastically at the class.

The class stared back blankly like stunned rabbits

caught in a blazing floodlight. I tried frantically to think of some way I could strangle Miss Tarango in front of twenty-five witnesses and make it look like an accident.

"Does anyone know the name of the famous novel with the main character called Ishmael in it?"

No, nobody knows, and what's more they don't care, so let's just move on and finish that register.

"No one? Well, what if I give you a clue? It's not set in the present day... and one of the other main characters is the captain of a ship."

Silence. Then a hand inched upwards. "Yes?"

"*Star Trek*, Miss?"

The class immediately erupted into laughter, but also secretly checked Miss Tarango's reaction on the off chance that the answer might just be correct. Miss Tarango laughed as if she appreciated the joke, but when she looked at Bill Kingsley, the author of the response, she knew that, sadly, there was no humour intended.

"It's Bill, isn't it? Well, not a bad effort, Bill. Well done for having a go. Maybe I should have said it was set on a sailing ship as opposed to a starship." Miss Tarango looked once more around the class. "Any other offers? No? Well, who's heard of *Moby Dick*?"

"Moby *what*, Miss?"

Muffled sniggers. It was Barry Bagsley again. There was no way he could pass up an opportunity like this.

"Moby Dick by Herman Melville, Barry," Miss Tarango said casually. "How many of you have heard of the story of Captain Ahab and his quest for revenge against Moby Dick, the white whale that took off his leg?"

Most of the class raised a hand with varying degrees of certainty and enthusiasm. Bill Kingsley stared into the distance as if he were already somewhere in a galaxy far, far away.

"But why was the whale called Moby *Dick*, Miss?"

More sniggers – somewhat less muffled this time. Barry Bagsley was not going to be put off that easily.

Miss Tarango appeared deep in thought, then replied thoughtfully, "To be honest, I really don't know, Barry. Names can be important or symbolic in books, so they often have a deeper meaning, but I'm just not sure if that's the case with the name Moby Dick. Perhaps Melville based it on an actual whale's name from historical records or perhaps it just seemed right to him. You know, just like your parents might have called you

Barry just because they thought you looked like a Barry."
She paused, then added as an afterthought, "In the same
way, I guess, they could just as easily have thought you
looked like a Dick."

A stunned silence hit the room. What? What was
that? What did she say? If Miss Tarango had intended
to insult Barry Bagsley, she showed no sign of it and
seemed blissfully unaware of the effect of her words.

Before the class could react, she had continued on
her cheery, smiling way. "Still, it's an interesting question,
Barry. Maybe you could do some research for homework
or try reading the novel and see if you can find the
answer there, and then maybe you might like to report
back to us in a class presentation. But for the moment
we'd better finish the register and go through the
morning bulletin before we run out of time completely."

There aren't many things that can shut Barry Bagsley
up, but being bombarded by words like 'research',
'homework', 'reading', 'report' and 'class presentation'
certainly seemed to do the trick. After that, the rest of
Tutor Group continued without disruption as Miss
Tarango bustled energetically about completing various
administration tasks and greeting everything and

everyone with equal enthusiasm. All the while the class watched and wondered.

But no one watched and wondered more intently than Barry Bagsley.

8.
FIVE AMAZING FACTS ABOUT ME

Fortunately, the only classes I shared with Barry Bagsley were Tutor Group each morning for 20 minutes, Citizenship with Mr Barker, the Deputy Principal, and English with Miss Tarango. Of course, morning tea and lunchtime could be tricky.

"Well, if it isn't Barbie Bimbo's pet student, Fish-whale Le Dick!"

Yes, Barry Bagsley was quite a wordsmith.

"I always said you were a Fish-whale, but I had no idea you were a famous Fish-whale."

Of course, at this point I could have informed Barry Bagsley that whales, since they were warm-blooded and suckled their young, were in fact mammals, not fish. However, this would have been like looking into the jaws of a frenzied shark and pointing out that it had some seaweed stuck between its teeth.

"Hey guys, look, it's the famous Fish-whale Le Dick. Hey, Le Dick, was that your girlfriend I saw you with yesterday or was it a white whale?"

Boom-boom.

"Girlfriend? Le Sewer Manure wouldn't have a girlfriend. He'd stink her out."

This gem came from Danny Wallace. Barry Bagsley was tutoring him in the traditional art of the creative put-down. He was progressing nicely.

"Maybe she was after some Moby *Dick* too?"

I think you can probably guess how the conversation went from there. Barry Bagsley and his scrum of supporters finally drifted off when a teacher appeared on yard duty.

My next encounter with him that first day of the year was in the lesson before lunch – English with Miss Tarango.

The class started with Miss Tarango outlining the unit of work for the term and somehow managing to make the assessment and even the poetry unit seem interesting. She talked a lot about the importance of language and how it could empower people. I wondered if that was true. Could language empower me to defeat Barry Bagsley? Perhaps I could drop a massive dictionary on him from a great height. I was enjoying this image when Miss Tarango handed out a sheet of paper to everyone headed *Five Amazing Facts about Me*.

"Write anything you like, but nothing boring. I don't want 'My hair is brown' or 'I have two sisters'. Think before you write. Be creative. Your five amazing facts could be serious or funny, important or trivial or whatever, just as long as they're true. For instance, maybe you've won some sort of award. Maybe you found a cockroach in a pie you were eating once or, worse still, half a cockroach. (Groans from the class.) Maybe you know or you've met someone famous or maybe you can touch your elbow with your tongue. (Many attempt this. No one succeeds. Bill Kingsley spends the next two weeks dedicated to this quest.) Maybe you have travelled somewhere interesting or maybe you have an unusual talent." (Quoc Nguyen twists his double-jointed thumb at right angles then bends it back to touch his wrist.

Gary Horsham turns his eyelids inside out. Donny Garbolo starts to belch the national anthem. Miss Tarango turns pale and suggests we all start writing.)

My list of Five Amazing Things about Me:
1. My sister is a genius.
2. My father played in a band called the Dugongs.
3. My mother is a councillor.
4. When I was an altar boy in Year Four I used to faint during the service.
5. I hate my name.

Miss Tarango said our answers would help her get to know us more quickly and to learn something about us. I didn't think she would learn much about me from my list, but I'd like to know what she learned about Barry Bagsley from his. As the lesson had progressed, Barry was returning to his old confident self. Even though Miss Tarango asked us to work quietly, Barry Bagsley was laughing and showing what he had written to his mates.

"Barry, if you're finished, you can hand that in now."

He took his sheet to the front, dropped it on

Miss Tarango's desk and returned, grinning, to the back of the room. As the rest of the class completed their lists, I watched as Miss Tarango read five amazing facts about Barry Bagsley. She seemed to study the sheet for a lot longer than it would have taken her to read it. No expression crossed her face. Then she laid the paper slowly on the desk and crossed her hands on top of it. She looked as if she was meditating. After a few seconds, Miss Tarango's head lifted, then turned towards Barry Bagsley. It reminded me of a warship locking its guns on to a target.

"Boys," she smiled sweetly, "if you're finished with your lists, pass them up and we'll just have time before the lunch bell for one more activity that I'm sure you'll all enjoy."

Folded sheets of paper began to rustle their way forward.

"Oh, and boys... just one more thing."

The growing murmur of sound within the room fell away.

"I'll need a volunteer," she said, scanning the class eagerly before levelling her sights on the lounging form of Barry Bagsley.

9.
NOW LISTEN CAREFULLY

When all the sheets had been collected, Miss Tarango stood up from her desk and moved to the front of the class. "Right. Now, for this activity I need someone who is strong-willed and brave, because he will need to meet the challenge of tackling the power of language. Have I got any takers?"

I glanced around the room. A few boys put their hands up. Barry Bagsley and his friends weren't among them. Neither was I. This was definitely a time to be a small target.

"A few brave souls, but what about the rest of you? Hope I haven't scared you off." Miss Tarango's eyes swept over the room like searchlights after escaped prisoners. I studied the surface of my desk intently.

"What about you, Ishmael? You look like you could handle the pressure."

I shook my head and smiled weakly.

"He won't do it – he's gutless."

"Well, I don't seem to remember seeing you volunteering, Barry, but perhaps I should explain the task a little more." With that Miss Tarango pulled the seat from the teacher's desk and set it up in the centre of the front platform. "Whoever volunteers will have to sit on this chair. His task will be to stay on the chair. My task will be to get him off the chair using only the power of language."

A general discussion boiled around the room.

Miss Tarango continued. "I am not allowed to order him off, threaten him, hit him, push him, or come in contact with him in any way, but before I walk around the chair three times, I guarantee he will no longer be occupying it."

Now the class exploded into a rabble of disbelief, accusations and questions.

"No way, Miss!"

"She's probably got a pin hidden somewhere."

"Can you tie yourself to the chair?"

Miss Tarango closed her eyes and held up her hands. "Boys, I've laid down the rules clearly. The time for talk is over. Who's willing to take me on?"

The reply was loud and immediate. "I'll do it."

"Barry?" Miss Tarango looked concerned. "I don't know if this is really your sort of thing. And besides, other boys volunteered before you."

"They won't mind."

Coming from Barry Bagsley, this was more an order than an opinion.

"Well, let's just check, shall we? Does anyone else want to volunteer? We can draw a name out of a hat."

Silence. Barry Bagsley, as always, got his way.

Miss Tarango appeared just a little flustered. "All right, Barry. I seem to have lost my other volunteers. Come out here, then."

Barry Bagsley ambled to the front of the room and stood beside the chair.

"Before you sit down, it's very important that I check a few things just as a precaution. Now, Barry, this is serious – tell me, do you suffer from any condition like a weak heart, high blood pressure or dizzy spells?"

Barry Bagsley rolled his eyes and shook his head. "Trying to scare me off won't work."

"I don't want to scare you off, Barry. I just want to be on the safe side, and I also want you to know that if you don't wish to go through with this, you can return to your seat now and no one will think any less of you."

We all knew she was bluffing, of course. She was a teacher. She was responsible. She was a girl, for crying out loud. She wouldn't do anything dangerous... would she?

Barry moved to the front of the chair. He looked out over the class, sneered and sat down defiantly.

"Right," said Miss Tarango, her voice suddenly as cold and expressionless as a prison guard's. "As I said, I won't speak to you or make contact with you in any way, but before I circle you three times, you will be off your chair. You must face the front at all times. If you look behind you, the challenge is lost. Do you accept that?"

Barry Bagsley nodded his head, but with a little less of his former arrogance.

Miss Tarango continued as if she were preparing

Barry Bagsley for execution. This was no time for dimples. "Now listen carefully, because *this* is the challenge. I will start at this point here," she said, stepping in front of Barry Bagsley's knees. "When I return to this point, that will be one circle and so on. By the time the third circle is completed, if you are still on the chair, you win. If, however, as will most definitely be the case, the third circle is completed, and you and the chair have parted company, then I win. Are you ready to begin?"

"What prize do I get when I win?"

"If you win, Barry," Miss Tarango said happily, "you can have the rest of the day off."

The room bubbled as if someone had just turned the air jets on in a spa. What? She couldn't do that. You can't just let people go home. Only the Principal, Brother Jerome, could do that. Why would she say something ridiculous like that? She's mad... unless, of course, she knew that she couldn't lose...

"Tell you what, Barry." Miss Tarango smiled sweetly. "I'm feeling generous. If you win, why don't you take the rest of the *week* off?" The spa was switched to turbo. "Boys, boys – thank you – quieten down now. What's all the hubbub about? Thank you. Now, Barry, are you ready to rock and roll?"

"I'm ready," said Barry Bagsley with a forced smile as his fingers tightened round the arms of the chair.

Miss Tarango surveyed the area around the chair. She frowned and shook her head slightly. A strange silence settled in the room. "Can you boys in the front row just move your desks back a little... a bit more... a bit more... That should be all right, but I usually like more space. We'll just have to hope for the best. Let's get started."

With that, Miss Tarango walked slowly in a clockwise direction until she was standing behind the chair. There she stopped and looked down at her hands. We couldn't see exactly what she was looking at because Barry Bagsley was in the way. Miss Tarango stood absolutely still for a few seconds before completing the first circle.

"That's one," she said flatly.

"Getting worried now, Miss? You're gonna lose ya bet."

Miss Tarango continued as if Barry Bagsley hadn't spoken and didn't exist. Her breathing had become noticeably deeper and slower. She moved around behind the chair for a second time. Again she stopped and glanced down towards her hands. Then she completed the second circle.

"That's two."

I looked at Barry Bagsley's face. It was set hard, and he gripped the chair as if he were rocketing towards the loop of a roller coaster. There was no way that he would leave that chair. Miss Tarango was doomed to fail. What was she thinking? She glanced nervously at the front row of desks and muttered something about workplace health and safety. The boys there automatically edged further back. She stepped behind Barry Bagsley and began writing on the board.

For a moment only the soft squeaking and tapping of a whiteboard marker filled the room as the entire class peered past Barry Bagsley's head to the words being formed in Miss Tarango's neat, even handwriting. Barry Bagsley's eyes danced and swivelled in their sockets as if at any minute they would spin around like symbols on a poker machine and reappear at the back of his head.

"Eyes to the front," Miss Tarango said coolly just as Barry Bagsley's head began to turn slightly behind her back. Miss Tarango finished writing and stepped a little to the side.

We all read what she had written. We all frowned.

Then Miss Tarango stood directly behind Barry Bagsley. She had only one half-circle to complete. She looked once again to her hidden hands and then slowly raised her left arm into the air.

Barry Bagsley watched mesmerised while all the eyes in the class moved to a point just above his head. The boys in the front row sat with mouths gaping, like a row of clowns in a sideshow alley. Behind Barry Bagsley, Miss Tarango had the cold stare of the Terminator as her fingers closed into a fist.

We knew she was bluffing, of course. But then again... maybe she realised Barry Bagsley had beaten her. Maybe she was desperate now and didn't know what she was doing. Maybe she was a fake. What did we really know about her, anyway? She could be a totally insane lunatic who had escaped from an asylum and was just pretending to be a teacher!

Miss Tarango's fist hovered over Barry Bagsley's head. She took in a deep breath. She seemed to be expanding so that her slight frame towered over the rigid form seated below her. Her eyes drifted up from Barry Bagsley's head to her fist. I held my breath, not knowing if I wanted her to do it or not. Then, when the tension was almost unbearable, Miss Tarango rotated her wrist, looked at her watch and turned to the class with a radiant double-dimpled smile.

When the end-of-lesson bell blared through the intercom, the whole class was jolted, as if they'd been stuck with electric cattle prods. Some boys gasped out loud. I was one of the gaspers. Bill Kingsley let out a squeal that would have been right at home in *Night of the Living Dead*.

Even Barry Bagsley flinched. But he didn't budge from his seat.

Suddenly Miss Tarango was her old self again. "Well, boys, we're all out of time, so we'll have to continue this tomorrow. Don't forget your English text for next lesson and your workbooks. Now pack up quickly and…"

But she was drowned out by a howl of objections.

Miss Tarango looked bewildered. "What's the problem?"

Barry Bagsley broke in rudely. "You haven't finished

the last circle. You have to finish the third circle and then I win. You can't back out now."

"But it's lunchtime, Barry. I don't want to hold up the rest of the class. We can do it tomorrow or perhaps another day. Good morning, everyone."

Barry Bagsley looked astounded. "What am I supposed to do?" he whined. "Sit here all night?"

Miss Tarango smiled pleasantly. "Well, yes, Barry, I suppose you do, because *that* was the challenge you accepted. If you don't believe me, it's right here on the board. You can turn around now and have a look if you want to."

Barry Bagsley swivelled around but maintained his grip on the arms of the chair. On the board was what Miss Tarango had written a few minutes ago – *Before I circle you three times, you will be off your chair.*

"You see, Barry, *this* is the key word here," she said, cheerfully underlining the word 'before' heavily. "Now, my part of the deal was to walk around the chair three times. I didn't say how *long* I would take to do that or *when* it would be completed. Maybe I'll do it tomorrow, maybe the next day or the day after that – maybe next year, who knows? And naturally, if you are still on the chair at the time, then you win. I promise you though, one day before I die, I will complete that last circle because, as I said, that's *my* part of the deal." Then Miss Tarango leaned in closer to Barry Bagsley and looked him right in the eyes. "Now *your* part of the deal is to *stay* on that seat *until* I do."

A groundswell of realisation rumbled around the class like a Mexican wave. When even Bill Kingsley's face eventually lit up in a rare display of comprehension, Barry Bagsley knew he was beaten.

"You see how powerful language can be, boys? Even a little word like '*before*' can hurt you if you don't treat it with respect and listen carefully. Now, before we all head off for lunch, let's give Barry here a *big* round of applause for having the courage to volunteer today and help with the demonstration."

Cheers and jeers mixed with laughter and clapping as everyone spilled noisily from the room. Miss Tarango had won more than just a challenge; she had won over the class – all except for Barry Bagsley, of course. He sat glowering in the teacher's seat while everyone filed out so that no one would see his unavoidable surrender.

Here are Five Amazing Facts about Miss Tarango:

1. Her dimples are deadly weapons.
2. Her smile is hotter than a laser beam.
3. She can make poetry sound exciting.
4. She's not afraid of Barry Bagsley.
5. She's definitely no Barbie Bimbo.

Supplementary Amazing Fact:
After just one day I knew she would be the best
teacher I ever had.

10.
HEY, BLUBBER BOY!

Miss Tarango might have won her battle with Barry Bagsley, but I was still fighting mine. Well, when I say fighting, it was more like I was cringing down at the far end of the trench while Barry Bagsley bombarded me with abuse. And to make matters worse, Miss Tarango's revelation about Moby Dick had provided Barry Bagsley with a whole new range of ammunition. Now his name-calling had taken on a decidedly nautical flavour.

"Hey, Blubber Boy!"

"Yo, Whale Dick!"

"How's it goin', Fish Paste?"

But there was something even more troubling about

Barry Bagsley. He was still burning with humiliation and resentment over the chair challenge. Not that Miss Tarango ever tried to rub in her victory. In fact, she never mentioned the incident again. At least I don't think she did – not intentionally, anyway. There was that one day when Barry was becoming very restless and was swinging and swivelling in his chair as if he was on a fairground ride.

"Barry, if that seat is uncomfortable for you, you're quite welcome to come and sit on the teacher's chair. It's padded."

That's all she said. Some of Barry's crew laughed and made comments, but Miss Tarango ignored them and continued to look at Barry with such genuine concern that no one was sure if she had meant to be funny or was deadly serious in her offer. It didn't really matter one way or the other. The thing was, it worked. Barry Bagsley immediately deflated like a punctured balloon while Miss Tarango smiled as sweetly as a rose till you really believed there couldn't possibly be any hidden thorns there that you might need to be wary of.

The problem was, however, with Miss Tarango out of reach of Barry Bagsley's anger and frustration, he had to find a closer, easier target. This is where I came into my own. Not content with chewing up my name and spitting it out in mangled, barely recognisable blobs, Barry Bagsley began to expand his repertoire of torment into other fields.

These included, but were by no means limited to:

- moving or hiding my bag, pencil case, calculator, books, hat or any other possession he could get his hands on, so that my day became one tedious, never-ending treasure hunt
- updating my homework diary with obscene drawings and suggestions, often involving Miss Tarango and whales
- leaving half-eaten sandwiches, sausage rolls and rotting pieces of fruit in my locker/desk/bag until everything I opened seemed to reek like a compost bin
- taking every possible opportunity to bump, push, jostle, shove, collide with, elbow, prod, dig, jab and shove me, so that I spent most of my lunchtimes careering around the playground and the school corridors as if I were trapped in some gigantic pinball machine.

All right, I know what you're thinking. Why didn't I stand up for myself? Why didn't I do something about it? But what would you suggest?

Threaten Barry Bagsley?

Look, Barry, I'm warning you, if you don't stop picking on me I'll make you listen to my father telling his how-Ishmael-got-the-name-Ishmael story.

Flatter him, perhaps?

Barry, Barry, Barry, you shouldn't be wasting your time just making my life miserable – you're so much better than that. Why don't you start a singing career? That way you can make millions of people miserable.

Appeal to his better nature, maybe?

Look, Baz old buddy, you're obviously a very sensitive and caring person. I think you would be great with animals. Have you ever considered working with orang-utans? Who knows? One day the orang-utans might even make you foreman.

Bribery, you say?

Look, B.B., have I got a deal for you. If you just leave me alone you can have all my worldly possessions – $3.75 in loose change and my 20 centimetre-diameter ball of used Blu-Tack.

Of course, I guess I could always plead with him while at all times maintaining my dignity:

Please, Mr Bagsley sir, please stop picking on me. Please, please, pretty please. By the way, would you like me to wash these feet of yours after I've finished kissing them?

Don't worry, I gave each of them serious consideration. But who was I kidding? Talking to Barry Bagsley was like trying to reason with an avalanche. You could say whatever you liked but you'd still end up being pummelled into oblivion. So I did nothing and I tried to convince myself that if I took him on, somehow I would be lowering myself to his level. Of course, the real reason had more to do with fear and the likely prospect of Barry Bagsley terminating my life with painful and extreme prejudice.

There was that one time, though, I guess I did stand up to Barry Bagsley... well, you know, sort of.

11.
INSIDE THE
MINCING MACHINE

It happened on the last day of first term. I was on my way home. I had just passed through the school gates and was about to turn down the long cement path that ran between Moorfield Creek and a row of six playing fields imaginatively referred to by everyone at St Daniel's as 'the Fields'.

Normally I had no trouble avoiding Barry Bagsley after school. If he wasn't tied up with rugby or cricket training, he always bolted from school on the final bell like an escaping prisoner. As a matter of survival, I made it my business to know as much about Barry Bagsley's daily routine as he did. That way I knew when I could leave school straight away, when it was wise to wait in the library (a place Barry Bagsley never voluntarily visited), what areas of the school grounds and playing fields to avoid and which route home I should take.

On this particular day, however, even with all available intelligence at my disposal, I had taken only one step on the path alongside the fields when I glanced up and saw Barry Bagsley and two of his mates 50 metres or so down the track. Luckily they hadn't seen me yet. All I had to do was turn back and take the long way home. And this is exactly what I would have done if I hadn't seen *him*.

I recognised the uniform straight away – the green and blue of my old school, Moorfield Primary. I'd missed him because he was so small – probably only in Year Three or Four – and the other larger boys had blocked him from my view. At first I thought it was some kind of game, because Barry and the other two, who I now recognised as Danny Wallace and Doug Savage, were tossing something between them while the little kid tried to catch it. Then I realised it was the boy's hat, and if it was a game, he wasn't enjoying it much because he was wiping tears from his eyes.

Every atom in my body told me that this was one of those times when the sensible thing to do was to make myself small. A few backward steps and I would be out of sight. Then I could forget all about Barry Bagsley and his mob. But that was just it. I could forget about the rest of them, but I couldn't get the kid out of my mind. I won't lie. I'm no hero. I *wanted* to turn around and run. I *wanted* to make myself small. I *wanted* to make myself disappear. The problem was, I had the terrible feeling that if I did, I might not ever be able to find myself again.

I don't know why, or what I thought I could do, but I found myself walking towards the triangle of grey uniforms and the small green-blue figure caught between them. I felt like a wooden puppet jerking and jumping as some madman operated the strings. It took every ounce of my concentration just to keep the movement of my arms and feet in order and stop them from tangling together and bringing me crashing to the ground.

Questions tumbled around inside my head like lottery balls. What am I doing here? Have I gone completely insane? Do I really think I can help? Why are my knees knocking together when I walk? Is it possible for a heart to pound its way through a chest? How did that prayer go that Grandma swore never failed? Is it too late to get the hell out of here?

"What d'ya know, it's Fish-whale!"

Well, at least I knew the answer to my last question.

"Hey, Le Spewer, wanna play some frisbee?" Barry Bagsley laughed and sent a floppy blue hat with a large letter 'M' embroidered on it sailing across to Danny Wallace.

The boy from Moorfield Primary made a half-hearted effort to catch it, but he had long since realised he was powerless. He looked at me with his red eyes and dirt-smeared cheeks as if I were just another tormentor.

Danny Wallace tossed the hat back to Barry Bagsley.

"What d'ya say, Piss-whale, you up for a game?"

I shook my head.

"What, you don't want to play with us? I'm shattered. Hey, boys, I don't think Manure here likes us. He doesn't want to play."

The other two laughed and pretended to be upset.

"Why don't you just give him back his hat?" There it was. I'd said it. There was no turning back now. I had strapped myself to the conveyor belt and was headed towards the mincing machine.

"Give back his hat?" Barry said in mock horror. "But we were having so much fun, weren't we boys?" Danny and Doug smiled like gangsters.

"He's not having fun. Just give him back his hat." I could hear the grinding and gnashing of steel on flesh.

"Well, Fish-whale, if you want him to have his hat back, why don't you just come and take it?"

Of course, what else would he say? It was as if we were caught in some ancient ritual where the lines and roles were always the same. What could I do? What could I say? Maybe if I were Wolverine from *X-Men* I could release the steel blades from my knuckles and slice Barry Bagsley into a pile of human onion rings. But wait, I don't have any super powers, do I? That's right, I forgot. I can't even bend steel in my bare hands or breathe out a tornado or turn people into ice just by staring at them. I can't even entangle them in a spider's web that squirts from my wrists. No, I guess I would just have to rely on the power of my enormous intellect to conjure up a devastating retort.

"Come on, just give him back his hat," I bleated.

Brilliant! I could tell Barry and his sidekicks were wilting under the barrage of my inspired words.

"What's the matter, Fish Dick? Here's your chance to be a hero. You're not scared, are ya?"

I said nothing. I did nothing. I was being ground and mashed into pulp.

"I tell you what. If you give us *your* hat to play frisbee with, I promise I'll give the kid *his* hat back."

No he wouldn't. I knew it and he knew it. Probably even Danny, Doug and the kid knew it. But I was so deep inside the mincing machine now, I had no choice but to hold on and wait until I was spat out the other end. I pulled my hat from my bag and gave it to Barry Bagsley.

"Great, two hats to play with – double the fun!"

I watched as my hat sailed across to Doug Savage, who plucked it casually from the air.

"Come on, you said you'd give it back," I moaned impressively.

"Oh no, I must have been lying. I'm going to burn in hell! Save me! Save me!"

Barry Bagsley has a fine sense of sarcasm. If only he could use it for good rather than evil.

They continued to toss the hats around. The Moorfield boy didn't try to stop them. Neither did I. What was the point? What if I did manage to catch one? What would happen then? Finally both hats ended up back in Barry Bagsley's hands.

"This is getting boring. You still want your hat back?" he said to the kid, who nodded without enthusiasm.

"Well, here ya go, then."

Barry Bagsley rocked back like a discus thrower and with a thrust of his arm sent the hat sailing high above the little Moorfield boy's head, over the embankment and down into the stagnant creek. "Oops," he said, placing his hand over his mouth. "It must have slipped. I'll try to be more careful this time. Your turn, Blubber Boy."

We all watched my grey felt school hat rocket right across the creek and lodge high up in a tangle of branches. Danny and Dougie applauded and cheered. Barry Bagsley doubled over with laughter. Where were those retractable steel blades when you needed them?

"Don't worry, mate," Barry Bagsley shouted back at the Moorfield kid as he swaggered off with Danny and Doug, "Fish-whale'll get ya hat. He loves the water."

The Moorfield kid and I didn't speak as we edged

our way down the bank to pluck his soggy hat from the green slime of the creek. And there were no words either as I struggled through the branches to retrieve mine. When we finally scrambled our way back up to the path, the awkward silence continued to hang around us.

"Well, I guess I showed them, huh?"

The Moorfield kid kept his eyes to the ground.

"Yep, I reckon they'll think twice before they try something like that again."

The Moorfield kid looked down at the path, where dark splotches of water fell from his hat.

"They should really consider themselves lucky, you know. Usually in situations like that, I lose my temper, turn green, expand to ten times my normal size and destroy everything in my path."

The Moorfield kid lifted his head slightly and looked up at me.

"Yeah, that's right. It's a bit of a bummer, actually. But recently I've taken one of those anger management courses because I was a bit worried I might really hurt someone. Besides, do you know how embarrassing it is to walk home with your school uniform and underpants in shreds?"

The Moorfield kid's lips moved a little.

"Last time Mum went ballistic."

The Moorfield kid spoke.

"Did *she* turn green?"

"No... a lovely shade of crimson, as I recall."

The Moorfield kid smiled.

"Look... don't worry about those guys, all right? They're morons. They haven't got enough brains to even appreciate how stupid they are. I'm Ishmael, by the way. Not according to that lot, of course, but they have this problem with names – particularly mine. Apparently they use up all their short-term recall just remembering to breathe. What's your name, then?"

"Marty."

"Well, Marty, unless you want to play another round of *Fetch the Hat from the Creek*, I suggest we both go home. Which way are you headed?"

We walked to the end of the Fields together sharing stories about Moorfield Primary before our paths divided. "Okay, see ya, Marty... oh, and if you ever need any help getting your hat thrown in the creek again, I'm your man, all right?"

"Okay... thanks," he said, and smiled shyly.

And that was the story of how I stood up to Barry Bagsley and his minions, rescued an innocent victim from the jaws of death and stopped the destruction of civilisation as we now know it. You'd think I would have been pretty pleased with myself, but walking home that day all I could think of was Barry Bagsley's grinning face and all I could feel were my knuckles aching on my clenched fists. It seemed like razor-sharp steel blades were straining to break through.

Part 2

I will not say as schoolboys do to bullies –
Take someone of your own size; don't pommel
me! No, ye've knocked me down, and I am up
again; but ye have run and hidden.

HERMAN MELVILLE, *Moby Dick*

12.
GEEK-SEEKING MISSILES

On the first day of the second term a new boy arrived at St Daniel's.

"Thank you, everyone, if you could just stop what you're doing and listen here now. We have a new class member joining us today. This is James – James Scobie. Now I'm *sure* that you will all make him feel *very* welcome here at the college." Miss Tarango's last words were spoken more like instructions than a statement of belief. When we got a good look at James Scobie, it was pretty obvious why.

It's not that the new boy was the Elephant Man or anything. In fact, he wasn't that different from anyone else, but he was just different enough to put him right in the danger zone – not so different that he could expect sympathy, but different enough to make Barry Bagsley's eyes light up.

To begin with, James Scobie was small and a little too neat. His hair was parted perfectly on one side and swept back from his forehead like a wave poised to break. The lines left by the comb's teeth were as clear as shoe prints on the moon. As for his clothes, it was as if his grandfather was his fashion guru. His socks were pulled all the way up and turned down at the top so that they matched *exactly*. His shirt was tucked tightly into his shorts, which rode high up over the little mound of his stomach. Apart from that, his skin was pale and looked as if it could be bruised by a strong breeze.

Yet all of that was noted quickly by the class and passed over. The thing that really held our attention was James Scobie's face – or rather, what he did with it. The face itself was nothing special – a bit chubby maybe, a smallish nose, a little too pink around the cheeks perhaps, but otherwise everything was where it should be. It's just that every so often James Scobie would screw up his mouth and twist it to one side till his eyes were swallowed up in a wrinkled squint and a hooded brow.

Then his mouth would straighten and his face would lengthen as his eyes popped open like that kid from *Home Alone*. Then the whole process would be repeated on the other side of his face. While this took place James Scobie's nose wiggled back and forth like he was trying out for the lead role in a remake of *Bewitched*.

The first time it happened, the class was taken by surprise. The second time, a shiver of laughter rippled through the room, but was cut off before it could grow by the hard edge in Miss Tarango's voice. "As I was saying, I have no doubt that all of you will do your best to make James welcome, just as we would want to be welcomed if we were starting in a new school."

Miss Tarango's eyes scanned the classroom and smiles dropped off faces like flies from a bug zapper. I glanced around at Barry Bagsley. He was staring at James Scobie like a kid who had just been given the Christmas present his parents had pretended they couldn't afford. I felt bad for James Scobie then. I knew what he was in for. Everything about him was a living, breathing 'Kick Me' sign. He might as well have come to school with a target painted on his chest.

I still feel bad about this. As I sat there looking at

James Scobie I thought my life might be better, that maybe James Scobie might take some of the heat off me. I know, not very nice, but you can't help what you think. The other thing I thought was that with all the attention he would get, James Scobie would be a dangerous person to be around.

"Now, I've checked James' timetable, and Ishmael, you and James are doing mostly the same subjects, so I've appointed you James' official buddy."

But...

"See that James knows where he is going and make sure you introduce him to his teachers, all right?"

But, but...

"I'm sure you'll be in good hands, James. Ishmael will be there to help you if you have any trouble."

But, but, but...

"And luckily there's a spare desk beside Ishmael, so you two can sit together during Tutor Group and English lessons and get acquainted. How's that?"

But, but, but... but it was too late.

James Scobie waddled down the aisle and sat in the seat next to me. We nodded at each other without speaking.

"Okay, everyone settle down and get yourselves organised and we'll read the notices shortly."

James Scobie reached into his bag and took out a pencil case and his student diary. He placed the diary in the centre of the desk, studied it closely, twisted his mouth and then straightened the diary slightly. He then removed three pens and a pencil from his case and laid them down one at a time before adjusting them delicately with his spidery fingers until the tips were in perfect alignment. Next he drew out a ruler, and, after a number of attempts, placed it parallel to the pens and pencil. Finally he opened the first page of his diary and pressed it neatly back. The long fingers of his left hand moved for the pens. He selected a blue one, removed the cap and scrunched up his face. Then he replaced the cap with a click and returned the pen to its position on the desk.

The new boy sat back twitching his nose like a rabbit, then leaned forward once more. His hand hovered over the red pen before settling on the black. He picked it up and slid off the cap. The pen lingered over the diary like a scalpel over a patient. James Scobie twisted his neck, stretched out his arms, straightened his shirt, made a minor realignment of his ruler, fiddled with his tie, patted down his hair gently, screwed up his face and poked the tip of his tongue between his lips. He tilted the diary to a minute angle. Then he tilted it back. Then he... left it where it was.

Finally he hunched forward on the desk and looped his left arm around until it looked like it might dislocate and, with his hand rotated almost backwards, rested the point of the pen beside the word 'Name' in his diary. With his face writhing and his tongue popping in and out like a moray eel, James Scobie began to write. When he'd finished, what was left on the page was a string of large, loopy letters that teetered backwards at an alarming angle and that were virtually indecipherable.

When I looked up, I discovered that Miss Tarango and the rest of the class were also mesmerised by the new boy's behaviour. I shot a look at Barry Bagsley. His eyes were almost popping from their sockets. I half expected to see a trickle of saliva running down his chin. There was no doubt that my 'buddy' was a prime target. Barry Bagsley had already locked in the coordinates and slipped off the safety switch. Soon he would be launching his geek-seeking missiles. No chance of a smart bomb here.

13.
THE BEST VIEW OF THE ICEBERG

As the class began to make its way from Tutor Group, Barry Bagsley's big head, with its mop of blond hair, lurched in beside me.

"Hey Piss-whale, got yourself a new girlfriend, I see. You make a *gorgeous* couple – Rat Boy and the Creature from Le Sewer."

With that Barry Bagsley gave my shoulder a friendly shove that stopped just short of dislocation before striding off, confident in the belief that he was still the king of observational comedy.

James Scobie watched him leave the room and stared at the empty doorway for a few seconds before turning to face me. "Friend of yours?"

"No."

An expressionless face gazed back at me and two small, dark brown eyes drilled into me like… well… drills. After some uncomfortable seconds, James Scobie twisted his mouth to the side until he looked like a plasticine figure that had been smudged by a thumb, then turned away and continued to pack up his books.

My first lesson after Tutor Group was Citizenship with Mr Barker in Room 301. It was James Scobie's first lesson too. And it was Barry Bagsley's first lesson. Not good. Because he took so long to pack up his gear, Scobie and I were the last to arrive. I glanced hurriedly around the room.

There was one spare seat in the back left-hand corner right in front of Barry Bagsley and Danny Wallace. Yes, I could sit there – if I had a brain the size of a pimple. There was an empty desk in the middle of the centre row. Getting better. And finally there was a space beside Bill Kingsley in the far row, right up the front near the teacher's desk. Perfect. After all, Miss Tarango didn't say I had to babysit James Scobie every lesson, did she? Of course, I wouldn't abandon him completely. I'd make sure he knew where he was going and help him out if

he needed it, but after that it was every man for himself.
I had enough trouble of my own with Barry Bagsley –
I wasn't about to make things worse.

I took a few steps into the classroom. The prospect
of sitting beside Bill Kingsley had never seemed so
appealing. Not that there was anything much wrong
with Bill Kingsley. I suppose he could be a bit… well…
vague at times. (The resident class comedian, Orazio
Zorzotto, once described him as "Still waters running
shallow", but that was a bit hard.) There were probably
only two things that struck you about Bill Kingsley.
One was that he was a sci-fi/fantasy nut and the other
one was his size. Let me put it this way, if there's
a tug-of-war competition and Bill's on your team,
then you don't need to have a vote for who should
be anchor.

I looked at Bill Kingsley's face. As usual he seemed
lost in his own little world, probably deep within Middle
Earth or the far reaches of the galaxy. The empty seat
beside him had my name on it. I was about to make
my move when I realised that James Scobie was saying
something to me.

"What… sorry?"

"I said, you don't have to sit with me if you don't want to."

Great, off the hook!

I watched as Scobie made his way to the spare desk in the middle row, where he began the excruciating routine of arranging his books and pens. Soon all eyes were drawn towards the centre of the room, where the small figure of the new boy sat fidgeting like a black dot in the middle of a target.

"Are you waiting for a personal invitation to take a seat, Mr Leseur?"

The rumbling voice of Mr Barker jolted the class into a flurry of activity. You didn't muck around when it came to Mr Barker. As Deputy Principal he was a busy man. His motto was, "You waste my time, and I'll waste you," and he lived by it.

I walked across the classroom. I looked at the seat next to Bill Kingsley. I looked at the seat next to James Scobie.

"Any time before the next ice age would be fine, thank you, Mr Leseur."

"Sorry, sir."

I sat down and quickly opened my book. Bill Kingsley

was gazing dreamily out of the window, probably fighting some desperate battle with orcs or aliens. I stared numbly at the vacant seat beside him. Don't ask me why I wasn't sitting in it. I turned to look at James Scobie next to me. He stared back with unblinking eyes as if he could read every thought in my head, then he nodded slightly and smiled, showing a row of small, neat teeth.

Oh well, I thought, if you're stuck on the *Titanic*, you might as well have the seat with the best view of the iceberg.

14.
BAD BARRY VERSUS TWITCHY JAMES

It was about 20 minutes into the lesson when the intercom buzzed and Mr Barker had one of his usual in-depth conversations.

"Yep. Right. Right. Yep. Righto. Right. I'm on my way."

Mr Barker was the school's 'go to' guy. If ever a water or food fight broke out in the playground or someone had money stolen or accidentally swallowed the lid of his pen (Bill Kingsley) or put his fist through a window because he didn't realise it was shut (Bill Kingsley again) or got his head stuck between the railings of the stairwell (yes, you guessed it) or if ever anyone had to be found, patched up, talked to, yelled at, disciplined, restrained or revived, then the inevitable cries would go up, "Get Mr Barker. Find Mr Barker. Go see Mr Barker. Try Mr Barker. Ask Mr Barker."

It seemed to me that Mr Barker was so busy dealing with everyone else's problems that he couldn't afford the luxury of having problems of his own. Therefore, whenever he was called away from class, which was often, his instructions came thudding down like a club.

"Right, listen up, you lot. I have to leave for a moment. While I'm gone read pages 38 to 45 and start working through the exercises at the end of the chapter. Leave your seat only if it is on fire. Don't speak unless it is to reveal your dying wish. Breathe only if it is absolutely necessary. I *will* return. I *will* check your work. I *will* be seeing you at lunchtime if I am not satisfied with both quantity and quality. Are we clear?"

We were very clear. Yes, you always knew exactly where you stood with Mr Barker – and that was anywhere he told you to. The class settled down to work as Mr Barker looked quickly around the room.

"Mr Kingsley, if you don't begin showing signs of productive life immediately, I will switch my laser from stun to destroy. Thank you."

Without further comment Mr Barker strode from the room. A few minutes later the first missile arrived. It shot over James Scobie's head, bounced across the desk and disappeared among legs and feet. The next one struck James Scobie on the back of the head, ricocheted into the air and lobbed on to his workbook. Scobie picked up the tight wad of paper and turned it over like a piece of forensic evidence.

Barry Bagsley's voice spilled across the room like a stain. "Hey, E.T., isn't it time you phoned home?"

Okay, listen to me now. I'm an expert in this field. This is what you do. Just pretend nothing happened. Mr Barker will be back soon. Forget about it. Just ignore it. And, whatever you do, don't turn around.

James Scobie turned around.

Oh. All right then, just take a quick peek, but don't make eye contact and definitely do not stare.

James Scobie stared.

Oh my god.

"What are you looking at, ya spazoid alien freak?"

Okay, now this is a bit like what Miss Tarango would call a rhetorical question. It doesn't require an answer. So don't answer it!

"I'm not sure," answered James Scobie thoughtfully, as if he were a contestant on *Who Wants to Be a Millionaire*. "As you point out, I'm new to your planet, but on the data available I'd say I was looking at some kind of rudimentary life form."

What?!

"Sorry," said Barry Bagsley with exaggerated concern, "I didn't mean to be rude."

What?

Somehow I think the difference between 'rudimentary' and 'rude' might have escaped Barry Bagsley.

"Definitely rudimentary," James Scobie said to himself.

By now everyone in the class was looking up from his book or twisting around in his seat to see what would happen next. Even Bill Kingsley had responded, but probably only to the mention of E.T.. Scobie and Barry Bagsley faced off against each other. It was like one of those old Western showdowns: Bad Barry Versus Twitchy James. You could almost feel the street emptying.

"What's your problem, Ferret Face? Something crawl up ya nose?"

James Scobie pushed his glasses up and frowned slightly.

"I suggest you turn around now, ya mutant, unless you'd like ya head smacked in. 'Cause I can smack it in for ya if that's what ya want."

James Scobie held Barry Bagsley's glare for a few seconds and then turned around and went back to work as if nothing had happened. Almost immediately a ball of paper the size of a small planet flashed into the side of James Scobie's head and left his glasses hanging from one ear. Cheers and whoops shot up from the back of the class.

"Hey, what's that stink? Is that you, Le Sewer, or has Rat Boy there just shat in his pants?"

James Scobie unhooked his glasses slowly and held them in his hand. His eyes rolled towards the ceiling as his mouth stretched first to the left then to the right. When he replaced his glasses, he leaned to the side of the desk, picked up the ball of paper, carried it slowly to the front of the class and dropped it in the bin. Every boy in the class followed James Scobie's movements like iron filings drawn to a magnet. He walked quietly back down the aisle. When he reached his seat, he kept going, and didn't stop until he was standing right in front of Barry Bagsley. Then he spoke calmly.

"When you said you could smack my head in, you were right, of course. I'd have little or no chance of stopping you. However, I should warn you that if you did take that course of action, I would immediately inform the appropriate authorities – Miss Tarango, Mr Barker, Brother Jerome – and my father. I would also have to insist that the police be contacted, since a 'smacked-in' head would certainly come under the banner of 'aggravated assault'. Naturally my father and I would be consulting a lawyer. By the way, I would suggest you do the same as soon as possible. I would also be checking myself in for a thorough medical examination in case compensation had to be calculated – medical bills, emotional and psychological damage, that sort of thing. At this stage, I don't think the media need be involved over an isolated incident. After all, I wouldn't want the school's reputation to suffer unnecessarily. But, if it happened again or there was evidence of other victims beside myself or indications of a history of violence and intimidation on your part – well, you know how the newspapers and current affairs programmes love that kind of hard-hitting investigative reporting." James Scobie stopped and pushed out his bottom lip. "So what I am saying is that *technically*, yes, you were right about being able to smack my head in, but I must say, for all the reasons I have just outlined, I would strongly advise against it. Now, as for me having 'shat' in my pants – by the way, do you think that's an acceptable form of the past tense? I'd like to see what the experts say on that. Anyway, I assume that you are implying by your comment *not* that I am incontinent, but rather that you believe your very presence has filled my body with such a volume of fear and trepidation that the only way I could accommodate it was by the involuntary emptying of my bowels. On this point I have to inform you, you are mistaken."

The class stared at James Scobie. Something wasn't right here. This wasn't the way things went. When Barry Bagsley threatened you, you backed down. That's just the way it was; the way it had always been. You couldn't just go changing things – just doing what you want. The whole room was one big furrowed brow. Something was happening here – we just weren't quite sure what it was. Perhaps that's what it felt like all those years ago during that football game at Rugby College in England when that Webb Ellis kid picked up the football and started to run with it for the first time. Perhaps everyone just stood there, blanked out by the shock realisation that there might be a whole other set of rules you could play by.

"You're mad, Turd Brain. Why don't you just run along before you wet your pants?"

Luckily, as far as Barry Bagsley was concerned, there was no situation for which an insult wasn't an acceptable response.

James Scobie gave Barry's comment due consideration before replying. "Well, of course, the individual is not the most reliable judge of his or her own sanity: only a psychiatrist could accurately rule on that. However, I don't *think* I'm mad. But there's one thing I *am* sure of: whether I'm sane or insane, I know I'm not afraid of you."

Barry Bagsley sneered, shook his head and pulled himself forward on the desk. Even though he was seated, his eyes still came level with Scobie's and his big-boned face hovered as menacingly as a death star. "Are you *sure* you're not afraid of me?"

"I'm sure."

"And exactly *why* is that?"

James Scobie squeezed his eyes shut, smudged his mouth around in a full circle, picked his glasses from his face and gave three wide-eyed blinks before settling them delicately back in position. He waited until his face fell still like the sea after a passing wave.

"Because I'm not afraid of anything," he said blandly.

15.
WHOOSH!

Not afraid of anything! This statement was greeted by hoots from Barry Bagsley supporters and general disbelief from the remainder of the class. I thought James Scobie had gone way too far now.

"Wooooooo," said Barry Bagsley, with his eyes bulging and his hands held up as if he were warding off some monster. "I think you might be telling a big fat porky there, Scobie boy."

James Scobie blinked twice and frowned. "Do I *look* scared to you?"

You see, that was the thing – he really didn't. Most people in a situation like that made the mistake of trying too hard to look brave or tough, but James Scobie looked as if he just didn't care. It was the same when he was introduced to the class. Everyone knows that one of the worst things in the world is to be the new kid. And the very worst thing about being the new kid is the moment when you have to stand in front of a room full of the old kids. The usual way of coping is to look at the floor or the teacher or out the window – anywhere, in fact, but at your new classmates – and pray that the torture will be over soon so you can scuttle to the relative safety of a desk. But James Scobie was different. In between the times when his face was twisting and stretching as if he were trying to swallow a blender, his small dark eyes looked over the class as if we were all new kids and *he* was right at home where he'd always been.

Barry Bagsley, meanwhile, was looking at Scobie as if he were something he'd just wiped from the bottom of his shoe. "Well, what's your secret, Superman? Made of steel, are ya? Got some super power or something? Wait, I know, you're really a boy wizard, right, with magic spells, and you're gonna wave your wand and change me into a toad."

"Not much magic needed there," said James Scobie with a smile.

A ripple of laughter broke out around the class. Danny

Wallace laughed the loudest but quickly wilted under Barry Bagsley's cutting glare before glowering at James Scobie as if he himself had been the target of the insult.

There was a battle going on before our eyes, but it wasn't like the Western shoot-out I had imagined earlier – this was more like a boxing match. In the black corner was Barry 'The Annihilator' Bagsley wielding the big blows that had left all his previous opponents bruised and bloodied and ducking for cover. In the white corner was James 'No Fear' Scobie letting the big punches whoosh past his face before moving in to prod and jab. Of course I didn't believe for a second that James Scobie could actually knock Barry Bagsley out, but he was landing some scoring punches and a room full of learned judges were marking them all down.

At this point, Barry Bagsley's patience (if there even was such a thing) had become as thin as the hair on my great-uncle Darryl's head. (Which was pretty thin considering that whatever hair he had was forced to stretch from just above his left ear, right across his bare spotty scalp to the other side of his head.) Anyway, where was I? Oh right, Barry Bagsley's patience, or rather lack of it. Barry Bagsley leaned forward again and jabbed his index finger in the middle of James Scobie's puny chest, where he tapped out an ominous beat as he spoke.

"Mate, if I *wanted* to, I could *snap* you in *half* like a *biscuit*. So if you're *not* afraid like you *say*, you *should* be."

Whoosh! Another Bagsley blow sailed past James Scobie's nose.

"Look," said James Scobie with a little impatience of his own, "I'm sure you are very tough and brave – after all, you have to look at yourself in the mirror every day..."

Jab!

"... and perhaps I *should* be afraid of you, because if it's true as they say, and 'a little knowledge is dangerous', then I suppose that you must be absolutely lethal..."

Jab!

Around the room, eyebrows were raised, jaws dropped and points were added to scoring cards. Barry Bagsley stared at James Scobie with the look of someone who knew he'd been insulted but wasn't sure exactly how or to what degree.

"... but I'm sorry," Scobie continued, unfazed. "I'm not afraid. It has nothing to do with you. It's because of this."

With that he brushed his hair up over his left temple. A big oval-shaped scar sat above his ear. He turned around so everyone could see it.

"What's that, then? Where they removed ya brain?"

Whoosh!

"No, if someone had his brain removed – even someone like yourself with as much grey matter as a spectrum..."

Jab!

"... it would result in a much larger scar than this. Although when I think about it, in a case like yours, keyhole surgery probably would be sufficient."

Jab!

"No," continued James Scobie casually, "this was the result of removing a brain tumour."

Silence crept around the room like a beaten dog.

"Aw, I get it," said Barry Bagsley, his voice dripping with contempt. "We all have to feel sorry for ya, do we, and hold ya hand and wipe ya bum for you 'cause you're sick, is that it?"

"Not at all," James Scobie said, as if the idea surprised him. "I'm fine now. The tumour is gone. It's just that there was a slight side effect to the operation."

"What, it turned you into a dork?"

Whoosh!

"No, if that were the case, we'd be best friends."

Jab!

"I don't make friends with freaks."

Whoosh!

"Well, keep trying. Perhaps they'll start to feel sorry for you and lower their standards."

Jab!

Barry Bagsley's face darkened. Things were getting ugly. Or in Barry Bagsley's case, uglier.

"Yeah, but what happened? You know, with the operation and the side effect and everything?" Barry glared again at Danny Wallace, who tried unconvincingly to cover his interest by adding quickly, "… as if I care."

"Well, as I said, the operation to remove the tumour was a success. But then one day I realised that something was different. I was different. I eventually worked out what it was. I could no longer experience fear. I tried to but I just couldn't do it."

"But what did you do, I mean, like how did you know…" Danny Wallace's voice trailed off into silence.

"The neighbours' dog made me realise," Scobie

continued. "He was a Rottweiler called Titan. He didn't take to people too well. One day I was walking past the neighbours' house. Someone must have accidentally left the gate open. I heard a growl, and when I looked up Titan was charging straight at me." James Scobie paused and looked Barry Bagsley in the eyes. "I just stood there and watched him. He was all teeth and slobber. He didn't worry me at all. When he was only a couple of metres away he launched himself at me." Scobie stopped.

"Well, go on, what happened? What happened then?" Danny Wallace didn't even bother about Barry Bagsley's reaction this time. Nor did the rest of the class.

"He was in mid-air and about to hit me when he was suddenly jerked backwards. I had no idea at the time that he was tied up. I couldn't understand why I hadn't been afraid. Then I thought about the operation. They warned me that it was a delicate procedure. It could easily have damaged my speech or movement. I began to think that maybe it had caused some other kind of damage. I decided to test my theory. I had always had a phobia about bugs – grasshoppers, cockroaches, and *especially* spiders – I couldn't bear the thought of touching them. I went home and caught some. I could let them run all over me. I didn't feel a thing. All my fears were gone."

The class sat in stunned silence, but Barry Bagsley wasn't going to take it lying down.

"Well, that's a *fascinating* story, Bug Boy, but if you've got no fear like you reckon, how about you climb up on the window sill over there and jump off? It's only three floors. That's nothing to be afraid of for a superhero like you. Go on, prove you've got no fear."

All eyes turned to James Scobie.

"If I plugged in a lamp and handed it to you, would you be scared of it?"

"Der, gee, I don't think so."

"Well then, if I told you to take out the bulb and stick your tongue into the socket, would you do it? Take your time, don't rush in with your answer."

"Course not," Barry Bagsley spat back.

"Well, just because I'm not afraid of jumping out the window doesn't mean I would do it. A tiny part of my brain that controls fear must have been damaged. The rest of my brain is fine. I'm not going to deliberately place myself in danger."

"Well, mate," said Barry Bagsley, standing up and

hovering over James Scobie like a guillotine, "that's bad luck, because you're in danger now whether you want to be or not and if you're Mr Fearless as you say, just stay right where you are, 'cause I'm going to count to five and if I'm still looking at your ugly mug, then I'm going to knock it off. Understand? Now these clowns might have fallen for all that tumour crap, but not me. So why don't you do yourself a favour and crawl back down your hole with the rest of the hobbits?"

The class took a collective breath. This was crunch time, and James Scobie looked as if he was going to be the crunchee. I was praying for him to back down. Barry Bagsley began the count like a death knell.

"ONE."

"Excellent start," said James Scobie encouragingly.

"TWO."

"You're going really well. Need any help with the next one?"

"THREE."

"If it's easier for you, you could just tap it out with your hoof."

"FOUR."

"There's no shame in using a calculator at this point."

"FIVE."

"Bingo!"

Barry Bagsley's eyes narrowed. I watched his hand mould into a fist and the muscles in his arms tighten. James Scobie blinked impassively. The room waited.

"All right, what's going on here? Why are we out of our desks? Mr Bagsley? Mr Scobie? Are we choosing partners for the next dance?"

Mr Barker's voice boomed into the room and shook it like an earthquake. "Well? I'm waiting."

James Scobie turned around slowly to face Mr Barker. "It's nothing, sir," he said. "This boy was just explaining the school's bullying policy to me."

Mr Barker raised his eyebrows and glared at Barry Bagsley. "Was he? Was he indeed? Well, Mr Bagsley and I have had our own discussions on that subject in the past, haven't we, Mr Bagsley? Yes, that's right. Glad to see you remember. Well, I trust that you made it very clear to Mr Scobie that we don't tolerate bullying in any form at St Daniel's and we take a very dim view – a very dim view – of anyone who practises it." Mr Barker looked around the room. "And I'm equally certain that if anyone here was bullied or anyone here witnessed another boy being bullied, they would immediately inform me or one of the other teachers. Everyone should feel safe at St Daniel's. I'm sure Mr Bagsley pointed that out to you, because that's what our bullying policy is all about, Mr Scobie. No one should be afraid here. Are you clear on that, Mr Scobie?"

"You don't have to worry about me in that regard," replied James Scobie. "I have every faith in the school's bullying policy, and after talking with Mr Bagsley here, I also have a great respect for the quality of education that the school provides."

"Really?" said Mr Barker cautiously.

"Absolutely. Mr Bagsley has just given us all a demonstration of how he can count to five…"

Jab!

"… and he didn't use his fingers once."

Upper cut!

The class laughed. Mr Barker frowned. James Scobie twitched. Barry Bagsley smouldered.

BRIIIIIIIIIING!

"All right, move out, you lot. I'll check those exercises tomorrow and that is a threat. Oh, and Mr Bagsley, could I have a word in your shell-like ear before you go?"

James Scobie and I packed up our books and drifted outside. I checked our timetables.

"James, we've got science next period over in lab three with Mr Kalkhovnic."

Scobie looked up at me. It was unbelievable. This guy had just gone the distance with 'The Annihilator'. I checked his face. There wasn't a mark on it.

"It's Ishmael, right?"

I nodded.

"Call me Scobie," he said, and smiled.

16.
THE UNEARTHLY EARDRUM-SHREDDING SHRIEK

Barry Bagsley gave James Scobie no more trouble for the rest of the week. But it didn't fool me. I knew something was brewing. I could smell it and I could hear it bubbling. I just didn't know what it was.

But the signs were definitely there. A few times, I noticed Barry Bagsley huddled in a tight circle with Danny Wallace, Doug Savage and some scrawny-looking boy from the year above. This was weird, because this particular boy didn't seem to have much in common with the rest of them. What I mean is, as far as I knew, he wasn't obsessed with torture and world domination. Besides that, he was a bit of a brain. I even remembered him winning some big award at assembly once. Anyway, he didn't appear to be all that pleased about being included in the Barry Bagsley inner circle.

Once or twice over the next couple of weeks I saw the older kid handing over boxes of various sizes which were hurriedly stuffed into school bags by the other three. Barry Bagsley would then send him off with some friendly slaps on the back that seemed more like an attack than a parting gesture, while Danny and Doug snickered and looked around slyly. Yes, something was brewing, all right, and in Tutor Group one Monday morning it boiled right over.

Three things struck me as strange that morning. Firstly, that smart kid from the year above handed me a note in the playground before school that said I had to go to the office. When I asked him why, he just mumbled something, shook his head wretchedly and left. The thing was, when I got to the office no one knew anything about it.

The second thing was when I got to Tutor Group

(later than normal because of my pointless office trip) Doug Savage was sitting on James Scobie's desk talking to Danny Wallace. This was strange, because those two usually had to be chased up by Miss Tarango to get to class. But there they were and Miss hadn't even appeared yet.

The third thing was that James Scobie was missing. He was always one of the first in, fussing about at his desk, organising, arranging, rearranging, adjusting, readjusting, shifting, shuffling, moving, edging, rotating and straightening every book, pencil and pen, piece of equipment, item of clothing and nearly every body part until his personal world was in order.

An uneasy feeling seeped through me as I moved to my seat and looked around the room. Everyone else was present – everyone except Barry Bagsley. This wasn't so unusual, since Barry Bagsley seemed to have set himself the challenge of being the last person into every lesson for the term of his school life. Having personal goals is so important. All the same, at the sight of his empty desk, a slithering dread began to uncoil in my stomach.

"What's up, Le Dick? You look a bit worried."

The maniacal grin on Danny Wallace's face made

me question the true level of his concern for my well-being. Beside him, Doug Savage stared at me. His small ball-bearing eyes seemed to have retreated deep in the dark caves of their sockets, as if they were tired of being bombarded by things that they couldn't comprehend.

"If you're worried about your little freaky mate, don't be. He's fine. See?"

Danny Wallace's finger was pointing out the window. I looked down into the playground. There by the bubblers, in deep conversation, were Barry Bagsley and James Scobie. Well, at least Barry Bagsley was in deep conversation. James Scobie could have been a statue if it wasn't for a twist of his mouth every so often. Then, after what seemed quite a long speech by his standards, Barry Bagsley thrust his hand forward. Scobie studied it for a second then reached out. After shaking hands vigorously Barry Bagsley threw his arm around James Scobie's shoulders and together they headed towards the stairs.

"Awww, that is just soooo *boodi*ful. Love will find a way. I feel all warm and fuzzy inside," Danny Wallace declared with a quaking voice. Doug Savage responded with a snort. This was bad. This was very bad.

"Okay, listen up, you clowns. I have an important announcement to make. A miracle is about to happen right here in Room 301. That's right, a *medical* miracle." Danny Wallace paused for effect. "In just a few seconds, right before your very eyes, little James Scobie will be given back his sense of fear. And you can all share in this wonderful occasion by just enjoying the show and keeping your mouths shut, right?" Then Danny Wallace leaned in so close to my face that he went all blurry. "Right?"

Soon after that two figures appeared at the door. Barry Bagsley gave James Scobie a friendly pat on the back, winked and headed for his seat, where Danny Wallace and Doug Savage quickly joined him. Around the class boys went through the motions of talking, unpacking books and doing last-minute homework, but everyone's attention was secretly focused on the small fidgety form of James Scobie.

Looking back, I suppose I should have done something or warned him in some way, but what could I have said or done that would have made any difference? Everything *seemed* normal enough, and though I knew *something* was going to happen, I had no idea what it was or exactly where or when it would unfold. I did try to catch James Scobie's eye, but he just nodded once, sat down and started to unpack his bag. It wasn't until he placed both hands on the lid of his desk and began to lift it that the memory of Danny Wallace sitting on top of it flashed into my mind and I finally knew at least *where* the danger lurked.

But it was too late. James Scobie had already straightened his arms and pushed up the lid.

A blur of wings exploded from within. It was like a scene from *The Mummy*, *Arachnophobia* and *A Bug's Life* all rolled into one. First about a dozen enormous green and brown grasshoppers catapulted themselves into the air, smacking into windows, leaping past startled faces and clasping their sharp spiky legs into unsuspecting hair, necks and limbs. This led to random outbreaks of what appeared to be the Mexican hat dance around the class.

Then three enormous stick insects the size of rulers roared into the air with humming, purple wings. Unfortunately one immediately flew up into the fan and was slung across the room, hitting the whiteboard with a sickening *Thwuug!* before sliding slowly and messily to the ground. One landed with a thud on Bill Kingsley's back and held on for all it was worth until Bill Kingsley ripped his shirt off in panic and flung it unintentionally over Doug Savage's head. This in turn caused a strange rapidly escalating growl to rise from Doug Savage as he madly tore the shirt from his head and sent it sailing out the window and into the playground three storeys below. The third stick insect continued to sweep around the room like a Black Hawk helicopter while everyone ducked and dived for cover.

As all this was happening, dozens of big dark brown cockroaches were spilling from James Scobie's desk, scuttling among stamping and pirouetting feet, diving into school bags or flying unpredictably around the room like fighter planes. Taylor MacTaggert, who sat in the desk immediately in front of James Scobie's, was laughing so hard at all the 'wusses' dodging and dancing around him that he failed to see until it was too late the three large spiders on the front of his shirt. He became aware of their presence only when the biggest one decided to seek shelter under his collar. At that moment Taylor MacTaggert did a fine impromptu impression of a Zulu warrior as he leaped madly into the air beating his head and torso like a frenzied drummer.

I would really like to be able to report at this point that I coped well in all this chaos, but the truth is, as soon as the first insects appeared, I leaped backwards from my seat, tripped over my school bag and landed on my backside on the floor. When I looked up and saw an advancing wave of spiders and cockroaches heading towards me, I scuttled backwards on my hands and feet like an upside-down crab to the far corner of the room. I was still taking refuge there when I finally looked up to see what James Scobie was doing.

About the same time, the rest of the class also began to regain some composure and, apart from isolated outbreaks of hysteria, they too were looking in James Scobie's direction. It seemed that in all the chaos, Scobie hadn't moved an inch. Now he sat motionless as the last of the cockroaches dived from his desk and scuttled to freedom.

Finally he lowered his arms. Then he turned slowly around and looked squarely at Barry Bagsley. The entire class stared at James Scobie's face. A spider the size of a saucer had spread itself over his cheek and neck. When Scobie screwed his mouth around and wrinkled up his nose, the spider's great hairy legs picked their way across his face before settling like a giant bullet hole over the left lens of his glasses.

Nobody moved or said a word.

If it wasn't for the unearthly eardrum-shredding shriek that came from Miss Tarango, we might have stayed frozen like that forever.

17.
THE EXCREMENT
HAS HIT THE FAN

Most people assume that Miss Tarango's unearthly eardrum-shredding shriek was produced in response to the last of the stick insects mistaking her neat, blond hair for a landing pad. Personally, I think the sight of Bill Kingsley with his shirt off might have been the real cause. In any case, it brought people running from all directions, and leading the cavalry charge, as always, was Mr Barker.

"Sweet mother of god, it's the plague of locusts!" he gasped in horror as he surveyed the classroom. It was quite a sight. Grasshoppers and spiders decorated the walls and ceiling and every so often startled cockroaches made erratic dashes across the floor. Meanwhile the stick insect that Miss Tarango had repelled with a mad flurry of hands before she fled down the corridor was now climbing shakily up the edge of the whiteboard, while the one that had tangled with the fan was lying like a wrecked umbrella on the ledge.

Mr Barker glared at the class. He ground out his words like a lorry in low gear. "I'm only going to say this once, so listen very carefully. You will have *one* chance and *one* chance only. I want whoever is responsible for this to… MY GOD, SCOBIE! GET THAT TARANTULA OFF YOUR FACE!"

James Scobie looked at Mr Barker and then crossed his eyes as he tried to examine the spider spanning his glasses. "Actually, sir, I think you'll find it's not a tarantula but a very fine specimen of a Mexican bird-eating spider. They're quite harmless, really."

"Scobie, I don't care if it's the spider equivalent of Mother Teresa. Just get that horrible hairy insect off your face!"

Scobie gently lifted off his glasses and placed them, with spider intact, delicately on his desk. "Technically, sir, it's not an insect, although many people make that same mistake. You see, insects' bodies are clearly divided into three parts or segments and insects usually have two pairs of wings and three pairs of…"

"Scobie!" Mr Barker's voice rang out like a warning shot. "If you say one more word, one – more – word, *you* will become an insect. Because if you say one more word, I will come down there and with my bare hands I will clearly divide *you* into three parts or segments and then before you know it, you will be flying, insect-like, out that door and down to my office. And guess what? You won't need two pairs of wings, Mr Scobie. Oh no. Because all the *thrust* you will need will come from my boot on your backside. Do I make myself clear, Mr Scobie?"

Scobie blinked his small glassy eyes and nodded.

"Right, now who knows where these insects came from?"

James Scobie raised his hand.

"Scobie, if you are about to tell me that that spider on your desk came from Mexico, I would recommend very seriously that you reconsider."

"No, sir, I was going to say that all the insects, and the *spiders*," Scobie added quickly, "came from my desk."

"From *your* desk, Mr Scobie?"

"Yes, sir."

"Do they belong to you, Mr Scobie?"

"No, sir."

"So are you telling me that you didn't put them in your desk, Mr Scobie?"

"Yes, sir."

"Well, in that case, Mr Scobie, do you have a theory on how the insects... and *spiders*... came to be in your desk?"

"No, sir. That remains a mystery to me."

"A mystery, Mr Scobie? Well, let me see if I can help you solve it."

Mr Barker rubbed his chin and paced slowly back and forth in front of the class, turning sharply towards James Scobie whenever a new hypothesis came to mind. "Tell me, Mr Scobie, do you think that it's possible... that the climatic conditions inside your desk just happen to be the next best thing to insect *and spider* Utopia, and maybe that's why bugs from all over the globe seem to be rushing to take up residence there?"

"I wouldn't think so, sir."

"No? Well, could it be... that your desk is not what it appears, but is in fact the opening to a wormhole in space that leads directly to the planet Insectoid?"

"Highly unlikely, sir."

"Then I suppose you would also discount the possibility that your desk is actually the portal to Hell... and these poor creatures are escaping the fiery furnace?"

"I'm afraid there's no hard evidence to support that notion, sir."

"Well then, tell me, Mr Scobie, is it just possible – and I realise that this is a bit out of left field – that maybe, just maybe, someone *else*, perhaps even someone in this very room, *put* all those insects, and other creatures that might appear to be insects but aren't really insects, into your desk because his disturbed and peanut-like brain perceived it to be something akin to a joke?"

Have I mentioned that Mr Barker had a black belt in sarcasm?

"What do you think, Mr Scobie? What is your considered opinion?"

"I think... that the only conclusion that can logically be drawn is that someone else put the insects and the *arachnids* into my desk," James Scobie replied seriously.

"Really? And would you have any idea just *who* might have done such a thing?"

James Scobie reached forward, gently tipped the big spider from his glasses and put them on. He looked around the class calmly before letting his eyes rest on Barry Bagsley. Then he turned to face Mr Barker. "If I knew for certain I would tell you, Mr Barker, but as I have no proof, I don't think it would be right to blame anyone just on suspicion."

"Very wise and very noble, Mr Scobie. I agree wholeheartedly with you. Justice must be seen to be done. So let's get our proof, shall we?" Mr Barker suggested happily. "Everyone… open up your desks and bags."

The end came very quickly for Barry Bagsley, Danny Wallace and Doug Savage. The shoeboxes with holes punched in the top, the empty jars and the paper bags were as good as an armoury of smoking guns. When Mr Barker pulled the last cardboard box from Danny Wallace's desk he took off the lid and shook it slightly.

"Well, well, well… another box with holes punched in the top and, if I'm not mistaken, insect excrement rattling around inside. To me, Mr Wallace, that could only mean one thing. Do you know what that is?"

Danny Wallace swallowed and smiled sheepishly.

"The excrement has hit the fan?"

"Oh yes." Mr Barker smiled back menacingly. "I couldn't have put it better myself."

18.
A BEAST, NO MORE!

After the insect (and spider) incident, Barry Bagsley's fortunes plummeted while James Scobie's rocketed skywards. It was as if they were on opposite ends of a gigantic see-saw.

The fallout from what Orazio Zorzotto labelled as 'Bug-gate' was that Barry Bagsley, Doug Savage and Danny Wallace were given a week's afternoon detention as well as being banned from school sport for two Saturdays, which meant no footy. For Barry Bagsley, this was the cruellest blow of all. The boy from the year above was found to be an unwilling participant in the whole affair. It seems Barry Bagsley had also recalled him getting an award in assembly once, but unlike me, he remembered it was for an amazing insect display that earned him first prize in a statewide science competition.

The boy, whose name was Jeremy Gainsborough, apologised to James Scobie, who dismissed it as nothing to worry about.

A few days later Scobie presented Jeremy with a replacement stick insect that was even bigger, more gaudily coloured and more bizarrely shaped than the one that had tangled with the fan. I don't know exactly what it was or where it came from, but it was enough to turn Jeremy Gainsborough into a gibbering idiot.

"But... how... who... where...?"

"Let's just say it flew off the back of a truck," was the only explanation James Scobie would provide.

As for Barry Bagsley, rumour had it that Brother Jerome had given him the 'last warning' speech. In any case, when he finally returned to class he was as sullen as a caged animal, a bit like the T-Rex at the beginning of *Jurassic Park* trapped inside that steel enclosure with a zillion volts of electricity zinging through the wires. Which was fine by me. The only trouble was, I kept thinking that when you watch a film like that, you just know that eventually, for some reason or another, someone or something will turn the electricity off. Still, for the time being at least, as long as I didn't stick my hand into his cage or fiddle with the high voltage switch, it seemed that Barry Bagsley was under control.

James Scobie, on the other hand, had become a bit of a cult hero. Even the biggest doubters began to think that maybe it was true and that maybe he really couldn't feel any fear. Certainly the image of him sitting calmly with a gigantic man-eating spider (the story tended to be embellished a little in the retelling) plastered on his face was very convincing. Yes, after only a few weeks at St Daniel's, James Scobie was the talk of the year. But it didn't end there. Soon he would have the entire school buzzing, and as far as Barry Bagsley was concerned, he would be untouchable.

It all started in the multi-purpose centre at the fortnightly school assembly. The assemblies were held right before lunch on Thursdays, so that if the need arose, as it nearly always did, Mr Barker could threaten us with something like, "If you can't sit still and listen politely and without comment, then we've got all lunchtime to practise." That usually did the trick.

On this particular Thursday, James Scobie and I had just come from Science and I was leading the way through the rumble of seven hundred boys to the rows of seats allocated to our Tutor Group. When I sat down, however, James Scobie was no longer with me, and I couldn't find him in the swirling flock of grey uniforms. I assumed that with his newfound celebrity, he had got caught up talking to someone, so I kept a seat for him and waited. But I was still alone when Mr Barker switched on the microphone with an amplified *Thook!*

"Right, settle down everyone."

The last of the stragglers were finding their places when I glanced up and saw Miss Tarango taking the register beside me. "James Scobie was here a minute ago, Miss, but I don't know where he's got to."

Miss Tarango smiled warmly. "I do," she said, pointing her pen towards the front of the hall.

I looked over the sea of heads to the stage, where Mr Barker bent his big frame close to the microphone and spoke like the voice of God in some Hollywood epic. "I'm waiting. I won't ask you again. We can always practise this at lunchtime."

The last murmur of voices was sucked up like dust

into a vacuum cleaner. Mr Barker's eyes drifted over the faces before him until the absolute silence hardened like concrete.

"Thank you, gentlemen."

It was only when Mr Barker stepped aside from the rostrum to pass the microphone to Brother Jerome and I ran my eyes along the row of teachers, student leaders and guest speakers seated behind them, that I saw the small frame of James Scobie perched calmly at the end. I turned and looked at Miss Tarango. She raised her eyebrows and dropped her jaw as if she had seen a ghost. When she smiled, I realised she had just been imitating my expression. In the end I had to wait through the entire assembly to find out what James Scobie was doing up there.

The main item on the assembly that day, after Brother Jerome's usual deep and meaningful address, Mr Barker's usual blunt and wide-ranging blast and a few mind-numbing reports from various teachers and student committee leaders, was a rev-up by the school captain and prefects for Saturday's big local derby rugby match, St Daniel's First Fifteen versus arch enemies Churchill Boys Grammar. Now to say that the St Daniel's versus Churchill rugby match was important is a bit like describing the end of the world as a break in transmission. No matter what else happened during the year – whether we lost every other football match in every age group or came last in the swimming and athletics or even if the average IQ of the entire school population plummeted to less than that of a worm farm – it would *still* be a good year if we could say, "At least we beat Churchill in the rugby!"

Tragically, no one at St Daniel's Boys' College had been able to say that for fifteen years, and *this* year our Firsts were languishing in the bottom half of the table while Churchill were undefeated on top with the premiership already secured. The only thing that stood between them and the coveted title of 'Undefeated Premiers' was the final game of the season against St Daniel's at St Daniel's.

Up on stage the school captain and vice-captain urged the school to turn out and support the team, and then they led us all in a rousing rendition of the college war cry.

By the time Mr Barker called on James Scobie to speak, the hall was bubbling and restless. "Right. Settle down. We have a final... I said, settle down! We have all lunchtime if we need it." Mr Barker scanned the hall. "Brad Willis. My office – now!" You knew Mr Barker was getting angry when he did away with verbs.

A lone figure skulked down the long aisle towards the back doors like a prisoner heading for the gallows. We settled down.

"Anyone else?"

There was no one else.

"Then we can continue. Our final speaker is James Scobie, who would like to talk to you about debating."

A rumbling groan rolled around the assembly. Mr Barker, who was halfway back to his chair, swivelled and glared. The groan retreated like a scolded dog. Mr Barker sat down, crossed his legs, folded his arms and stared straight ahead. Scobie walked in his strange upright style to the rostrum, his stomach and hips arriving slightly before the rest of his body. He stepped up on the small platform and the microphone pointed into his forehead like an alien probe. Laughter poked its nose tentatively back into the hall. Mr Barker uncrossed his legs and peered into the mass of boys, stretching his back and neck up like a periscope.

James Scobie pulled down the microphone and

looked calmly at the assembled school. His mouth
slewed to one side, and then slid across to the other
before thrusting upwards. This time the laughter broke
free and scuttled and slid around the hall like an excited
mutt on slippery lino. Mr Barker sprang to his feet and
took a step forward. The hall hushed.

James Scobie began to speak.

What is a man,
If the chief good and market of his time
Be but to sleep and feed? A beast, no more!

Scobie pounded on the rostrum. The whole assembly
stared. Mr Barker stared. James Scobie waited and then
his strong clear voice rang out again.

He that made us with such large discourse,
Gave us not that capability and god-like reason
To fust in us unused…

In the audience heads began to turn. Around me I saw
eyes filled with questions. Questions like, "Who is this
guy and why is he speaking in tongues?" But before

anyone had time to put his bewilderment into words, James Scobie continued.

"Gentlemen, these lines from *Hamlet* remind us that if we don't utilise our power of reason, if we let it fust or decay in us unused, if we don't exercise and challenge our minds, then we are no better than beasts who simply spend their lives sleeping and feeding. I bring this to your attention because last year, to our shame, no teams from St Daniel's competed in the Schools Debating Forum. This year we want to change that. Here at St Daniel's we are rightly proud of our fine sporting tradition, but we need also to test ourselves on intellectual battlefields. We need to engage our minds. This is the role of debating. Now some of you may feel that debating is for wimps. I'm here to tell you that you are wrong. Research shows that most people are more afraid of speaking in public than they are of dying. Debating is not for wimps. It's for boys with courage. That's right, courage – the courage and commitment to stand up and perform under pressure. If you disagree, then put your hand up now, and volunteer to debate me on the topic at our next assembly."

A murmur shuffled around the gym. Scobie waited. No hands went up.

"Gentlemen, we are not looking for the world's best speakers. Those skills can be developed. We want boys with the courage and commitment to do St Daniel's proud. If you are such a person, then come to the meetings scheduled for next week, and if you have any questions at all please see me, or Miss Tarango, who has generously volunteered her time to be debating coordinator."

The assembly remained silent a moment and was about to give its usual half-hearted applause, but James Scobie wasn't quite finished yet.

"Finally, if I may, I would like to recite a few verses I've written for another group of boys who will also need to show courage and commitment when they represent the college this Saturday against the might of Churchill. The poem is called *We Are St Daniel's Men*."

The murmuring started to gain momentum again. James Scobie waited until it subsided. Then a defiant voice boomed from his small frame.

> *We wear the mighty blue and white*
> *We play it hard*
> *We play it right*

Will we lie down? No! We will fight
With all our might and courage.
We'll step with pride upon the field
We will not bend
We will not yield
We'll strive until our fate is sealed
A backward step not taken.
And should our efforts seem in vain
We won't relent
We'll strive again
Till we have overcome the pain
And set our course for glory.
And when the battle's been and done
Win or lose
We'll stand as one
United in the race we've run
And no foe will deny us.
They'll see that we're St Daniel's men
We don't give up
We don't give in
With courage forged in a lion's den
We stand proud and defiant.

For a second there was silence. Then the school captain let out a "Woo!" and stood up and began to clap. Around him and throughout the hall the applause, shouting and whistling grew like a landslide.

Soon the audience was on their feet and they stayed that way, clapping and cheering while James Scobie folded his notes and made his way back to his seat. Not even Mr Barker suggested we should settle down.

Scobie's poem and his stirring delivery were the talk of the school. Even Mr Hardcastle, the sports master and coach of the First Fifteen, a man not noted for his subtlety and appreciation of poetry, saw its potential and asked for a copy. "We'll use some of the words and whip up some banners and posters. That should stick it up those Churchill girls!"

Like I said...

Coach Hardcastle even asked James Scobie to come to the game as his 'secret weapon'. We had no idea what he was talking about. Scobie agreed, anyway, and asked me to come along as well, and that was how I got to witness, up close, the final stage of James Scobie's rise to fame.

19.
THE MAGNON

Scobie and I arrived at the main oval well before kick-off, but the stands and surrounding grassed areas were already almost full. Fortunately, Mr Hardcastle had arranged a spot for Scobie down near the fence behind the St Daniel's reserves' bench, and luckily I was able to squeeze in as well.

Coach Hardcastle's face was set like rock. "Stay right there, Scobie, in case I need you. You might be our last hope," he said solemnly before marching off briskly to the changing rooms.

15 minutes later the crowd roared as the two teams ran on to the field and lined up facing each other.

While the referee spoke to the players and checked their boots, the St Daniel's and Churchill supporters shook the stand with their school war cries.

I looked over both sides. The game hadn't even started, yet somehow the Churchill team seemed bigger, stronger, faster and more skilful. There was only one positive I could see for St Daniel's, and that was that Frankie Crow, Churchill's most feared player, was not on the field. Thankfully, the rumoured knee injury appeared to be a reality.

Finally the coin was tossed and the teams separated for the kick-off. The first half was hard and grinding. There was no doubt that the St Daniel's team were playing the game of their lives, but even though their defence was outstanding, they struggled to match the skill and pace of their opponents. With 5 minutes of the first half to go, Churchill had already scored three tries to one, but thanks to some wayward goal-kicking on their part and a lucky intercept try to us in the dying seconds, St Daniel's went to the break trailing by only two points.

Coach Hardcastle quickly bundled the team into the dressing room. As he passed us he shouted, "Scobie, get ready to do your stuff." We both wondered exactly what his 'stuff' was.

We soon found out. Before half-time had finished, Coach Hardcastle hustled the St Daniel's team back on to the field. Then he came over to the reserves' bench, handed Scobie a copy of his poem and a microphone and said earnestly, "We need you, son. I want you to give it everything you've got, Scobes old pal. Let it rip, boy. Don't leave anything in the tank. Do you hear me?"

Scobie furrowed his brow, pushed his bottom lip forward and waddled out to where the team was lined up in front of the grandstand. Then he turned to face the crowd and drew the microphone to his mouth.

If the reading at the assembly was stirring, this one was electric. Scobie was inspired. He paced in front of the team like a circus ringmaster, and his voice echoed around the ground as he hammered out the words of his poem as if he was chiselling them on stone. When he shouted out the line, "Will we lie down?" he pointed the microphone to the crowd and a deafening and defiant "No!" blasted back at him from the grandstand like a sonic boom. Later, when he boldly declared, "We will not bend. We will not yield," huge banners and posters rose from the stands with the words emblazoned on them, and soon more followed with "We don't give up. We don't give in."

By the time Scobie was through and the opposition had finally made their way on to the ground, the St Daniel's supporters were on their feet cheering deliriously and the team was champing at the bit.

Coach Hardcastle might have had a lot to learn about tact and political correctness, but no one could teach him anything about motivation and putting the wind up the opposition.

And his plan seemed to be working. In the second half, the St Daniel's boys tackled like demons. Churchill came nail-bitingly close to scoring on a number of occasions, but a blue and white jersey always arrived at the last second to stop the try or force a fumble.

But for all their heroics in defence, St Daniel's still needed to score to win the match. As the game wore on, this seemed less and less likely. Most of the time St Daniel's were scrambling on their own try line. They just couldn't seem to make it into the opposition half. Not only that, for all the heart and courage they were showing, they were tiring rapidly, and, more and more, another Churchill try seemed inevitable.

With just over 5 minutes left and the score line unchanged from half-time, Coach Hardcastle took his last throw of the dice. It was his final substitution. To everyone's amazement, Juan Corianna – our lone try scorer from the first half and the team's crack goal kicker – was pulled from the field and replaced on the wing by Peter Chung.

Now don't get me wrong – everyone liked Peter. Although his English was scratchy, he was always joking and laughing and he was a great hit, especially with the younger boys. The problem was, he wasn't such a great player. He had heaps of enthusiasm and he was surprisingly strong for his size, but he couldn't really tackle and he wasn't quite up with all the rules. Once, after St Daniel's were on the end of a 40 – nil drubbing, Peter asked a teammate cheerfully, "So which was the team that won?"

Chungy did have one major asset, however, that kept him in the side. If he caught the ball (and I'm talking a jumbo-sized 'if' here), he could run faster than anyone St Daniel's had ever seen in its seventy-two-year history. Coach Hardcastle's tactics were obvious. If we could get the ball to Peter Chung in a bit of space, with his blinding speed he just might be able to pull off a miracle try. The big question was – would Churchill try to exploit Peter Chung's weakness in defence?

We didn't have long to wait before finding out that the answer to the big question was 'Yes'.

Almost immediately a huge form draped in a blanket stood up from the Churchill bench. As the blanket dropped from its shoulders, a despairing groan rose from the St Daniel's supporters. It was Frankie Crow, with his left knee gripped in white strapping. As we watched with dread, Cranky Frankie Crow – otherwise known as 'The Magnon', as in the Cro-Magnon Man – began to warm up.

But there was worse to come. When Magnon got on to the paddock he didn't take up his usual position in the forwards. He lumbered straight to the wing. He was right in front of us, a metre from the sideline, and opposing him with a beaming smile was Peter Chung. It was the mismatch of the century. Chungy was short and only slightly built. His biggest muscles were in his calves and in his smile.

Crow stood like a block of granite. From the waist up the Magnon's torso arched out like an inverted pyramid on top of which his neck-less head seemed in the process of being swallowed by his massive shoulders. His biceps were so huge that his arms stuck out at 45-degree angles from his sides. When he walked, his legs rubbed together and the muscles on his thighs clicked into fearsome bulges with every step. Orazio Zorzotto claimed that Frankie Crow was so brutal, he was once sent off for gouging his own eyes. (Did I mention that he was also fast over a short distance and had good hands?)

Frankie Crow set his sights on the chirpy, bouncing form of Peter Chung. Peter's face danced with a crazy mixture of joy, excitement and sheer terror. For his part, the Magnon had only ever mastered two expressions – the 'death stare' and, if he was in an exceptionally good mood, the 'I'm-going-to-pound-you-to-within-an-inch-of-your-life-but-let-you-live stare'.

The weird thing was that Churchill didn't even have to score to win. They were still two points ahead and we looked as if we had no hope of crossing their line or even getting close enough to kick a goal. But Churchill being Churchill, I guess they just wanted to rub our faces in it by scoring in the dying minutes. And that's exactly what they looked like doing.

The strong Churchill pack controlled the ball and attacked the far side of the field, dragging more and more weary St Daniel's defence across and leaving Peter Chung on the near side more and more isolated and exposed. There was less than 2 minutes to go and Churchill were only 5 metres from our line when the inevitable happened. Churchill changed the direction of the attack, and with two long passes the ball was on the other side of the field thudding into the barrel chest of Frankie Crow. The Magnon's big hands swallowed the ball up greedily, and he began to rumble towards the try line like a gigantic boulder careening down a mountainside.

There was only Peter Chung to stop him.

It was all over. An entire grandstand drew in its breath and waited. Parents covered their children's eyes. The Magnon had been 30 metres out when he received the ball. By the time he had travelled 10 metres he was at his maximum velocity. A hush fell around the ground like a sheet being pulled over a corpse. Suddenly, beside me, James Scobie was on his feet, and his voice blared out across the field like a trumpet call. "We don't give up! We don't give in!"

Immediately Peter Chung's face lit up. His eyes narrowed crazily and he gritted his teeth and grinned like a madman. He shouted out what we all assumed were his dying words. "We don't give up! We don't give in!" And then he set off towards Frankie Crow as if he were exploding from the starting blocks of the Olympics 100-metre final. When Frankie Crow and Peter Chung met head-on at the 10-metre line, everyone expected Peter Chung to be bashed to the ground, mashed underfoot and flattened like a cartoon character beneath a steamroller.

And that's precisely what happened.

Never in my life had I seen anyone or anything go as quickly from standing upright to flat out like a pancake as Peter Chung did that day. The crowd winced and let out a sympathetic "Ooooooo!" But one other thing happened. Just as Frankie Crow was finishing using Peter Chung's body as a treadmill, the tags of his left boot got caught up in the straps of Peter's headgear. For a moment the Magnon was thrown off balance, and as he tried to adjust his step, his foot hit the ground at an awkward angle. His ankle wobbled. His knee twisted. A sickening *Click!* shot through the air. Frankie Crow dropped the ball, clutched at his knee and crashed to the ground like a detonated building.

Amazingly, when the Magnon spilled the ball it ended up in Peter's hands. Chungy gazed at it groggily for a moment, then sprang to his feet and started running. He went from unconscious to warp-speed three in two seconds flat. Most of the Churchill players were on the other side of the field expecting a Magnon try. There was only the fullback to beat. When he got to him, Peter Chung stepped off his left foot, stepped off his right foot, stepped off his left foot – and then accelerated to the right at full speed. The Churchill fullback was left stranded with his arms outstretched, wobbling from side to side like a zombie from a horror film. Meanwhile Peter Chung raced under the posts and leaped about wildly with the ball above his head while the entire St Daniel's College and supporters screamed hysterically at him that he had to ground the ball for the try.

Coach Hardcastle's face was purple, and he added quite a few descriptive words to his instructions about grounding the ball in order to emphasise the urgency of the situation. Miss Tarango, who was sitting nearby, did a lovely imitation of a traffic light changing to 'Stop'. In the in-goal area, Peter Chung cupped his hand behind his ear as if he was straining to hear what the roaring crowd was saying. Finally, as the Churchill players galloped desperately towards him, he gave an exaggerated nod, smiled knowingly, tapped the side of his head with his finger, bent down and gently pressed the ball into the lush green turf.

The St Daniel's supporters exploded with joy. Coach Hardcastle slumped to his knees and wept. The entire St Daniel's team charged at the madly grinning figure beneath the goal posts. And Peter Chung, having survived the murderous rampage of the Cro-Magnon Man, ended up with a cracked rib and mild concussion, thanks to the appreciative embraces of his teammates.

Not that it stopped him grinning away as they carried him in triumph around the field. When the excited huddle arrived at the main grandstand, Coach Hardcastle pulled James Scobie from his seat and two big St Daniel's forwards hoisted him onto their shoulders to continue the lap of honour.

As they paraded him before the delirious home crowd, James Scobie waved and held up his own handmade sign, twirling it around slowly. On one side it proclaimed proudly, 'St Daniel's men: Courage forged in a lion's den!' and on the other it said simply, 'Debating meetings next week. Check the noticeboard. St Daniel's needs you!' As I watched Scobie being swept away by the throng of supporters I wondered how many boys would take up his debating challenge.

There was one thing for sure. As much as I'd come to admire James Scobie, I knew that there was no way that I would be one of them.

20.
DANCING POLES
OF JELLY

"Ishmael, I've put your name down for our year's debating team."

It was the Monday morning following St Daniel's famous victory over Churchill. James Scobie blinked up at me calmly.

"You what?"

"I've put you down for the debating team," he said again, as if he was making some passing comment on the weather.

"You *what*!" I said more loudly, trying to indicate the level to which my hysteria was rocketing. I stared at Scobie in shock. I shook my head in horror. Had he gone completely mad? Could he hear himself? Did he have the faintest idea that what he was really saying was, "Ishmael, I've put you down for standing completely naked in front of a room full of strangers while your heart is ripped out through your mouth and your skin is peeled slowly strip by strip from every centimetre of your body."

"Is there a problem?"

A problem? Was there a problem when someone on the *Titanic* sent out for ice?

"You can't... I can't... I'm... hopeless... I'm... I'm no good... no... no way... I can't do it."

What I was trying to explain to him was that I would rather have my tongue stapled to my forehead than take part in debating. I would rather whisper sweet nothings into the cauliflower-like ear of Frankie 'The Magnon' Crow than stand up and talk in front of a crowd. I would rather be the only Ishmael in the Barry Bagsley School for Clones than to be within a million light years of public speaking. Do you see what I'm getting at? I wasn't really that fussed on the idea.

"You'll be fine. I can help you."

"No... no... it wouldn't... you... you don't...

I couldn't... it's just... I... I... I can't... I... I..."

Now you see why Scobie wanted me in the team – I had a way with words.

"You could sit out the first round of debates until you felt more confident, then join in after that."

He made it seem so easy, but he had no idea what it was like for people like me. Did James Scobie know what it was like to stand in front of a class while his face felt like it had just exploded in flames and his ears sizzled like deep fried potato wedges? Had he ever had his legs turn into dancing poles of jelly and his kneecaps leap about like lotto balls? Had he ever felt his hands swell into giant air balloons until there was nowhere to hide them and his eyelids become so heavy that they forced his head on to his chest and made it impossible to look up?

How could anyone like Scobie, who could address an entire assembly or a stadium full of people as easily as talking to himself, know what it was like to be someone like me? I'm like that guy in the film we watched in English with Miss Tarango – *Dead Poets Society* – Tim, or Tod, I think his name was. You know, the one who's too shy to say his poem to the class and so Robin Williams, who's playing the teacher, just tries to get him to yell something out in front of everyone – a 'wild barbaric yawp' he calls it, or something weird like that – but the kid can't do it because the pressure of all those eyes is just killing him. Well, no disrespect to the actor, but I could have played that role with one hand tied behind my back.

I knew that James Scobie would never understand, and so I didn't waste my breath even trying to explain. "Look, I'm sorry... I just can't do it."

"What if you didn't have to speak?"

I glanced up to see if he was joking, but he looked back at me blankly.

"What do you mean?"

"What if you were in the team but didn't have to debate?"

Now there was an interesting proposition, and it opened up exciting possibilities. If I could do that, perhaps I could join the swim team but not swim or play first-grade rugby for St Daniel's from the sidelines. But hey, why stop there? I could ace all my exams without actually sitting for them, leave school and find a highly paid job without working, marry a beautiful girl without meeting her and settle down and have lots of kids without...

"What do you say?"

"Don't get me wrong – I like the idea, but wouldn't that kind of... defeat the purpose?"

"Not at all. We can have up to five members in the team. That gives us three for each debate, plus a reserve, plus you."

"But what would I do?"

"You can be our research man and help with the preparation and the writing of the speeches. Look, you might have some trouble with talks, but when it comes to writing, I'd say you were probably the *second*-best student in English," he said with a slight smile, "*and* you're smart, *and* unlike some of our fellow classmates, you are actually aware that the school has a library and, more amazing still, you know what it's for and how to use it. Ishmael, I won't make you speak – I promise that – but to put it quite simply, I need you."

I trusted James Scobie and I wanted to help him, but I couldn't stop the panic from rising inside me. It was like when I was little and my father took me out in deep water for the first time. He said he wouldn't let go of me and I believed him, but I still tried to burrow myself into his chest like a giant tick.

"But I don't know anything about debating."

"I'll teach you. Besides, there's a big workshop on at Moorfield High – we'll go to that."

"But what if more than five people want to be in the team – and all of them are actually willing to debate?"

"Then I guess you're off the hook, aren't you? Look, the meeting's Wednesday at lunchtime. Just come along and help me with it – maybe take down names or something, and we'll see what happens. It couldn't hurt, could it?"

"No, I suppose not," I said warily as I sensed the water darken and grow colder around me.

Of course I was wrong. It could hurt very badly indeed.

Part 3

There are certain queer times and occasions in this strange mixed affair we call life when a man takes this whole universe for a vast practical joke… and more than suspects that the joke is at nobody's expense but his own.

HERMAN MELVILLE, *Moby Dick*

21.
GO TEAM!

Scobie's campaign to establish debating in the school had some success, particularly in the year group below us, where there were enough volunteers to form three teams. Unfortunately there was little or no response from the rest of the school.

The last scheduled meeting was for our year group. On Wednesday at lunchtime James Scobie and I arrived at the meeting room early and waited.

I didn't really know if I wanted anyone to walk through the door or not. It was a real numbers game. If no one came I'd be in the clear, but I'd feel a bit bad for Scobie. If at least four other people showed up I'd still be in the clear, but then Scobie would have his debating team. If only two or three others turned up, Scobie would get his team and I'd be in it. What I needed was either a famine or a flood of volunteers. Just as that thought settled in my mind, Ignatius Prindabel peered around the doorway like a dog on lookout duty and asked, "Debating?"

When Scobie nodded, he stepped awkwardly into the room and sat down.

Ignatius Prindabel always reminded me of an old man, I guess because he was thin and kind of stoopy and his hair started too far back on his forehead. Sometimes I had the crazy thought that he was really a pensioner working undercover for the government, you know, like a spy checking up on teachers or a stooge for the drug squad. But what I could never work out is why they would be using pensioners. Were they cheaper? Were they the only ones with the time to spare? In the end I decided it was more likely that Ignatius Prindabel was just a weird-looking kid like the rest of us.

As I added his name to the list alongside mine and Scobie's, I wondered what sort of debater Prindabel would make. There was no doubt that he was one of the smartest boys in the year. He was a living, breathing search engine for facts, figures and dates: he saved them up and treasured them like gold coins. His particular areas of speciality were maths, science and history. He rarely set foot into the realms of the unknown. Not only was Prindabel the type of person who flatly refused to think outside the square, he insisted on thinking in the precise geometrical centre of it. Ignatius Prindabel liked his world and everything in it to be as practical and predictable as a set square. If you could measure it, calculate it, prove it, define it, classify it, chart it, label it, dissect it, preserve it, place it on a timeline, stick it in a box or pin it to a board, then it found a home in the Prindabel universe.

I knew that cold hard facts would certainly come in handy in a debate, but the trouble was, I hadn't really ever heard Prindabel string together much in the way of conversation, let alone deliver a speech, and he seemed to get on better with a computer or a dissected rat than he did with people. In a world that Miss Tarango kept on insisting was limited only by our imaginations, Ignatius Prindabel always looked to me like someone in a straitjacket. Somehow, debating and Prindabel didn't exactly seem like a match made in heaven.

"How come you're putting your name down for debating, Ignatius?"

"I require more 'social interaction skills'," he said as if he was talking about some plant that needed more fertiliser.

"Oh… right. And what makes you say that?"

"My mother," he said, as he pulled out a calculator and began stabbing in numbers.

Suddenly the door burst open. "Yo dudes, this the debating gig? Hey Scobster, your prayers are answered – The Big Z has answered the call! What? This all we got? No problem. Probably just as well we didn't get a big turnout. Wouldn't want it turning in to a mass debate eh? Mass-debate? Geez, you're a bit slow on the uptake, aren't youse? When do we start? What's the topic? Hey, Prindabel, my bro! Is it true that some hot chick asked you for a date and you said, 'July 20, 1969 – first moon landing'? Man, is it warm in here or am I on fire?"

A lost and despairing expression clawed its way across Ignatius Prindabel's face. It was the same look that appeared whenever Miss Tarango mentioned poetry.

The new arrival was Orazio Zorzotto, more commonly known as Razz, Razza, The Razz, The Razzman or Zorro. Only Orazio himself ever used the name the Big Z. At least I could understand why Razza would turn up. Debating would help him with his goal of becoming either a politician or a stand-up comedian. Obviously he had come to hone his public speaking skills.

"Hey, Scobes, we'll be up against some chick schools, won't we? Yeah? Cool, I'm in!"

Then again, maybe the Big Z had ulterior motives.

A few moments later the large form of Bill Kingsley drifted into the room.

"Is this the Chess Club sign-up?"

"No," Scobie said, "I think you'll find that was on Wednesday… the week before last."

"Close, Kingsley, but no cigar," Razza said. "Did it take you all that time to find the room? Still, you're only a couple of weeks late. You'd think they would've waited. What is wrong with society today?"

"What's this, then?"

"Debating. Are you interested?" Scobie asked.

Bill Kingsley looked slowly at each of us. "All right," he said, and sat down.

"What!" This was too much for Razza. "You come to join the Chess Club and end up on the debating team? You *do* realise there is a bit of a difference, don't you, Kingsley?"

Bill Kingsley shrugged but made no effort to reply.

Razza leaned over from his desk and placed a friendly hand on his shoulder. "Look, you're into all this science-fiction UFO space crap, aren't you? Well, tell me... is it possible that maybe sometime in the past some of those weird alien dudes might have beamed you up to their mother ship and removed your brain to study but like, accidentally dropped it or stood on it or something? Or perhaps, you know, they just took your brain completely and they replaced it with something else, like maybe a sponge or a block of wood or some weird alien sludge? Or maybe they dissected you to examine all your body parts but when it came to putting you back together they got your brain and your bowels mixed up, you know what I mean? Think, Kingsley. Try to remember. It's very important. Do you recall flashing lights at all? Little green men? An empty feeling in your head?"

Bill Kingsley just stared back but said nothing.

"Orazio, we haven't got much time, so if you

don't mind we might get started?"

"Just trying to help," Razza said, holding up both hands towards Scobie as if to show that he was unarmed. Then he flopped back in his seat, where he began to quietly drum out a frantic beat on the lid of his desk while his legs bounced around like pistons.

"Well, it doesn't look like anyone else is turning up," Scobie continued, ignoring the manic performance beside him, "so we're it. Congratulations, you've been selected for the debating team."

Razza leaped from his seat. "Oh my god. I can't believe I made the top team. Oh my god. OH – MY – GOD!" Razza gushed. "I would like to thank the Lord, my parents, my dog Mitzy, my pet cockroach Filthy and all the little people I had to trample over to get here. But most importantly, I'd like to thank everyone who didn't show up for the meeting. I love you guys – I really couldn't have done it without you. Thank you… thank you… thank you…" And with that Razza slumped forward on his desk, seemingly overcome with emotion.

I must admit, I couldn't help smiling a bit – that is, until I saw the complete lack of reaction from anyone else in the room.

"Continuing on," Scobie said cautiously, while fixing Razza with a steely glare, "on these sheets I'm giving out, Miss Tarango has put down everything you need to know about debating, as well as the dates and venues for the first four rounds. You will note, that in order to go on to the semi-final and finals, we will need to win at least three of our first four preliminary debates."

"Piece of cake, what with Billy Boy here firing on all cylinders – how can we lose?"

Scobie again ignored Razza and went on.

"I don't suppose any of you have debated in competition before? No? Well, I have for the past two years, so basically I will be your coach. Miss Tarango will also help out when she can, but she'll have her hands full with the other teams. As you can see, our first debate is in just over three weeks. We should have the topic on Monday. Also, this Saturday, they are running an all-day debating workshop at Moorfield High. Ishmael and I are going, and if anyone else can attend, that would be good."

"Sorry," Prindabel said, "… Scouts."

"What about you, Kingsley?" Razza asked politely. "That doesn't clash with your Victims of Alien Abductions meeting, does it?"

"No, I'm going to the cinema. Mega *Lord of the Rings* marathon – all three parts, back to back – goes all day."

"That's great," Razza said encouragingly. "If we ever get the topic *That hobbits are stupider than dwarves*, you'll be our main man. Hey, Scobie, will other schools be there at this workshop thingo, you know, like chick schools and stuff?"

"I would imagine so. Everyone's invited," Scobie replied patiently.

"Cool. I'm there. The Razz will be *in* the building!"

"All right, we'll schedule a meeting for next Tuesday at lunchtime in this room, if that's not a problem with anyone."

"Pop that down in your Star Fleet commander's log, Kingsley, so you don't forget. Oh, and Kingsley, my man, it would be lovely if you could aim to get there at least somewhere within the same light year, okay?"

"Finally," Scobie said, waiting for Razza to look his way, "I'd just like to remind you that debating is all about teamwork. And that means working together, supporting and helping each other and presenting a united, cohesive front."

With James Scobie's words ringing in my head, I looked around at my fellow debaters.

Orazio Zorzotto had circled all the girls' schools on his sheet and was now in the process of giving each of them an RBR (Razza Babe Rating) out of ten. Ignatius Prindabel had covered the back of his handout with mathematical computations and was secretly plugging numbers into his calculator. Bill Kingsley had half-finished a doodle of a spaceship and was now gazing ahead dumbly as if he were having some vague but unnerving recollection of flashing lights and little green men.

Go team!

22.
THE FOUR STEPS
OF EFFECTIVE
REBUTTAL

The debating workshop at Moorfield High that Saturday could have been a very useful and informative experience. However, it turned out to be just another step along the road towards my ultimate and most extraordinarily thorough humiliation.

It was the day I first saw Kelly Faulkner. Not that she noticed me, of course. I was just one of the thirty or so students and a handful of teachers that showed up for the workshop. But I noticed her, and unfortunately Orazio Zorzotto also noticed me noticing her.

"Hey, Leseur, stick your tongue back in – you're starting to dribble."

It was the lunch break. Orazio and I were waiting outside a classroom for Scobie, who was still inside, deep in conversation with one of the presenters from the morning session.

"What?"

"Come on, you can't fool the Razz. You've been perving on that weird chick in the red T-shirt all day," he said, jerking his head towards a group of girls clustered under a tree.

"What? I wasn't perving at anyone."

"If you say so."

"And she's not weird," I shot back, perhaps a little too quickly.

"Woo... Sorry, didn't mean to pay out on your girlfriend."

"Girlfriend?! What are you talking about?"

"Look, don't get me wrong. I don't blame you. She is *kinda* cute in a... freaky sort of a way. It's just, she's not my type, you know."

I didn't really know, but I guessed that Razza's type would be someone along the lines of Britney Spears or Paris Hilton. You know, the sex-goddess-next-door type.

"You should go and chat her up."

Oh yes, that'll happen. What a terrific idea. I could just wander over and say, "Excuse me. My name is Ishmael Leseur... Yes, I agree, it *is* an interesting name... did you know it's also the name of a debilitating syndrome? Anyway, I thought you might be dying to leave all your friends and join a complete stranger in a conversation. Or, on the other hand, you and your friends might prefer just to stare at me like I'm a slobbering three-headed zombie before dissolving into hysterical laughter while at the same time pointing and using what Miss Tarango refers to as 'apt descriptive phrases' like 'complete loser', 'absolute dork' and 'brain-dead moron'."

"Look, Razza, I don't even know what you're on about. I haven't been *looking* at anyone, I don't want to *talk* to anyone, and I'm not *interested* in anyone, okay?"

"Really? Then how about telling me the Four Steps of Effective Rebuttal."

"What?"

"The Four Steps of Effective Rebuttal. Go on – we just had a talk on them."

"What's that got to do with anything?"

"Well, it's just that the speaker-dude in there only

mentioned those steps about a zillion times *and* put them up on the OHP. So unless you had your mind completely fried by some babe in a red T-shirt during the whole talk, you'd have to remember them, wouldn't you? So come on, lover-boy, I'm waiting."

"This is stupid. I don't have to do this!"

"*Can't* do it, you mean. Look, I'll make it easy for you: just give us a couple of the steps… they don't even have to be in order… how about one, then? Oh my god. Don't tell me you can't even remember one? This is worse than I thought! Quick, help me pluck this arrow from your heart before it's too late!"

Suddenly Razza had both hands on my chest and was wrenching at my shirt. "Arrrrrrrrrrrrrgh! Curse you, Cupid!"

"Get lost!" I said, finally struggling free. "I bet you can't even remember them yourself."

Razza froze immediately, stood to attention and then droned out the steps like a programmed robot. "First – say what the opposition said. Second – say why they are wrong. Third – say what your team says. Fourth – say why you are right."

"So I wasn't listening. So what?" I mumbled as

I tucked my shirt back in. "What does that prove?"

"It proves to *me*, Ishmael my man, that at the very time when you should have been burning into your memory fascinating information from the world of rebuttal, you were in fact," and here Orazio leaned uncomfortably close to my ear and whispered as if he was sharing a delicious secret, "logged on to the website of luuuuuurve!"

"You're mad," I said, pushing him away. "You realise that, don't you? You should be locked up. They shouldn't let people like you into the community with normal people without strict supervision."

Razza cleared his throat, thrust out his jaw and spoke to an empty bench in front of him. "Ladies and gentlemen, *chair*, I give to you the Four Steps of Effective Rebuttal. One – my love-struck colleague Ishmael said that I was mad. Two – my randy associate is wrong, because he has no medical training and therefore is incapable of making such an outlandish diagnosis. Three – I say my besotted teammate is just accusing me of being mad in order to cover the fact that he has the terminal hots for a certain red T-shirt girl but doesn't want to admit it. And four – I am right, because if anyone is qualified to make such a diagnosis it is I, because I am the Razzman, and the Razzman is the doctor of luuuurve!"

I looked at the beaming face before me. I wanted to kill him... slowly.

"I pretty much reckon that'd be game, set and match to me, Ishmael old pal. And just in time. Here comes our fearless leader."

Finally some sanity.

"Herr Scobie, I am sorry to report that I no longer think that Comrade Leseur here is fit to be a member of our party. He hasn't taken any notes from the morning session, and under intensive cross-examination I have discovered to my horror that he doesn't even know the Four Steps of Effective Rebuttal. I'm sorry, but his mind is just not on the job. He's being a fool to himself and a burden to society. What on earth do you think has got into him, Herr Scobmeister?"

Scobie looked at me then turned to Razza. He squinted and twisted his mouth to one side. At last, Orazio Zorzotto was about to be put in his place.

"Probably spending too much time staring at that girl in the red T-shirt?" Scobie replied.

Razza thrust both arms into the air and threw his head back. "Woo-hooo! Yes! The Scobster slam-dunks it in one! You da man, Scobie baby. You – da – man!"

Orazio Zorzotto danced around me, poking me in the ribs and messing up my hair. Looking back, I realise that I should have killed him then while I had the chance. Once the jury had all the evidence, I probably would have got off with a few hours of community service.

23.
TWO BLUSHING PENGUINS

For the rest of the debating workshop I concentrated on taking as many notes as possible and on keeping my attention firmly fixed to the front. If ever I wavered and let my eyes drift anywhere near a certain red T-shirt, Orazio Zorzotto would either clasp both hands over his heart and look to the heavens with fluttering eyelids or seize his chest and gasp in silent pain as if an arrow had just struck him.

That night as I lay in my bed I thought about what Razza had said. It was stupid, of course. I wasn't in love. I mean, how could I be? I knew nothing about Kelly Faulkner except her name and I wouldn't have even known that if it hadn't been for the name tags they gave us. (I pinned mine under my jumper just in case someone had a bad reaction to it like Barry Bagsley's.)

No, I definitely wasn't in love. That was for sure. All that Romeo and Juliet stuff – making dopey faces through fish tanks or saying weird things like, "my lips two blushing penguins are," or whatever it was – just didn't happen in real life. Though I suppose Razza had a point in a way. I admit I was *looking* at Kelly Faulkner quite a lot, but I definitely *wasn't* perving. Kelly Faulkner wasn't even the perving type. She was different. Not freaky or weird like Razza said, just different. She wasn't one of those girls who seem to spend all their time just being beautiful and then don't have any time or energy left to be anything else. No, I wasn't a *perver* and she wasn't a pervee and I wasn't in love. So what was it about her? Why couldn't I keep my eyes off her?

I thought about the first time I saw her – *really* saw her. It was during that first session. She was part of a debate that the presenter put together as a demonstration for us. When she stood up to speak, the thing I noticed straight away about her was her eyes. How weird was that? I never pay attention to people's eyes. Most people

I talk to could have grapes hanging from their eye sockets and it wouldn't strike me as strange. And as for colour... who notices stuff like that? Not me.

But with Kelly Faulkner's eyes it was different. I couldn't help but notice. They were so pale blue that it looked like they were made of ice – but not cold like ice – just clear and shiny, and when she smiled her cheeks pushed up and made her eyes disappear into narrow slits that seemed to sparkle with light... or something like that. As I said, I don't really take in much about people's eyes.

But noticing things about someone's eyes isn't love, is it? It's more like... interest or... curiosity. Like how I found it *interesting* that Kelly Faulkner had tied her hair back into two small pigtails and that she wore a red clip in the shape of a butterfly and that she had a few light freckles around her nose. And how I was *curious* about the way she tucked some loose strands of hair behind her ear and the way the back of her neck was slightly pink from the sun.

And I suppose I was even more *interested* and *curious* whenever she smiled and I had to stop myself from smiling right back at her because she looked so happy.

And I guess it was the same when she spoke and her voice made me think of bubbling water or when she got her words mixed up and she giggled and bit her top lip and made a goofy face and yet still somehow managed to look... well... perfect. You see, that was the strange thing about Kelly Faulkner. Everything *about* her was perfect – even that silly red T-shirt with the black outline of an Indian chief on the front. After a while you couldn't imagine her wearing anything else. I guess that's what made her so *interesting* and why I couldn't stop watching her – she was just so perfect at being herself.

That night I had a stupid dream where Kelly Faulkner and I were friends and we'd go over to each other's houses and talk and joke around and once she laughed so much her eyes crinkled up into slits and she had to hold her stomach and rest her head on my shoulder until she recovered. Like I said, really stupid, but the thing was, it seemed so real that when I woke up on Sunday morning, just for a second or so I thought it *was* real. But then I remembered, and it was gone. Just like when you turn off the TV and all the colours disappear and everything just goes grey and silent.

For most of Sunday I wandered around looking for

something to do. I tried watching TV in the lounge. I tried listening to music in the snug. I tried kicking a ball around the garden. I tried reading on the balcony. I even tried doing some homework in my room. But everywhere I went seemed grey and stale – just one more place where Kelly Faulkner wasn't. As a last resort I even tried talking to Prue, but she said she was halfway through *War and Peace* and wanted to finish it before the next day.

At last I went to my room and flopped back on my bed. Surely Razza couldn't be right after all, could he? It was impossible. It didn't make sense. What would he know about love? Wasn't *he* the one who was perving at all the girls yesterday and giving each of them a RBR? Then it dawned on me. Of course – the Four Steps of Effective Rebuttal! I would destroy Razza's stupid ideas and give him back some of his own medicine.

Let's see. One: Razza says I'm in love with Kelly Faulkner. Two: This is totally false because… because… be… suddenly I found myself thinking about the shape of Kelly Faulkner's blue jeans and the way her lips parted when she smiled and her cute white teeth.

An awful pain ached in my chest. I lay there and

waited for it to pass. There was nothing else I could do. I was on the receiving end of a mega download from the website of luuuuuurvc.

24.
MY BROTHER, MY CAPTAIN, MY KING!

I decided that my best course of action was to try not to think too much about Kelly Faulkner – what was the point in torturing myself, right? Instead I focused on debating. The way I thought about it, the chances of me getting anywhere with Kelly Faulkner were infinitesimal, whereas the chances of us winning a debate were only microscopic. I decided to stay in the realm of exceedingly slim possibility.

By Monday we had our first topic – *That our leaders today rely more on image than actions* – but from the start it didn't look too promising.

The problem was, despite Scobie's best efforts, I don't

think we had quite grasped the idea of teamwork. While he desperately tried to keep everyone on task and I attempted to take down any relevant points, Ignatius tossed up chunks of useless information that exploded like fireworks, distracted everyone's attention and then disappeared without a trace, Bill sat comatose as if he'd been deep frozen in some space pod that was at that very moment hurtling towards some distant outpost of the universe, and Orazio divided his time between complaining about the topic, cracking jokes, sharing his insights on 'hot chicks' and insulting the rest of us.

Here is just a small sample of what I mean.

Orazio: What a stupid topic. What side are we on again?

Scobie: Negative. We have to argue that our leaders *don't* rely more on image than actions – that their actions are just as, if not more, important than image.

Orazio: But that's crap. Why do *we* get the crap side?

Scobie: It doesn't matter what you believe. You can make a case for both sides.

Orazio: Can we ask the other team if they want to swap?

Scobie: No.

Orazio: Well, that sucks. First debate and we get stuck with the crap side.

Scobie: Look, we can't change, so let's try to examine the topic. We need to look at who 'our leaders' are. For example, does the topic just refer to political leaders like the prime minister?

Orazio: Him? Mum reckons he's an idiot. They should give him the push.

Prindabel: Did you know that the shortest serving Australian prime minister was Francis Forde? He lasted only eight days in office.

Orazio: Eight days? Kingsley took longer than that to finish his last Maths test.

Scobie: Well, that's interesting, Ignatius, but it doesn't really help us with our side of the argument.

Orazio: The crap side.

Scobie: Bill, any ideas?

Kingsley: About what?

Scobie: Well, can you come up with any examples
              of leaders who have relied more on actions
              than image?

Kingsley: There's Aragorn, I guess.

Orazio: Who?

Kingsley: Aragorn, from the *Lord of the Rings*. You
              know, that bit in *The Fellowship of the Ring*
              where Boromir doesn't want Aragorn as his
              leader but they fight the Urak-hai together
              and when Boromir is dying he changes his
              mind and says to Aragorn, "I will follow
              you, my brother, my captain, my king."

Orazio: Geez, thanks for that, Bill-bo. You've been
              such a big help. Now why don't you toddle
              off back to the Shire and have a big sleep
              while the rest of us deal with reality, okay?

Prindabel: New Zealand was the first country to give
              women the vote.

Orazio: You haven't got some nerd's strain of
              Tourette's syndrome, have you, Prindabel?
              What the hell has New Zealand giving
              women the vote got to do with anything?

Prindabel: Well, *Lord of the Rings* was filmed in

New Zealand and we were talking about prime ministers and government.

Orazio: Have you been sleeping with your head in the microwave again?

Me: Come on, Razz, let's get back on the topic, hey?

Orazio: Me? Me? Kingsley's the one that's going on like he's been smoking too many hobbit pipes, and any minute now Prindabel will tell us that the seventh prime minister of Australia was Tolkien's love child. And as for your gems of wisdom, Leseur – here, I've written them all down on this postage stamp – double-spaced in an extra large font, and look – there's still loads of room for your photo.

Scobie: Well, Orazio, perhaps you can give us the benefit of your understanding of the topic?

Orazio: Okay, Scobes, I'd love to. As a *leader* with the *ladies* I'd say that the really hot chicks like a bit of *action* but having a cool *image* is also important. Fortunately the Razz can provide both.

Prindabel: Then how come I've never seen you with a
'hot chick', Orazio?

Orazio: How come I've never seen you with a
human being, Prindabel?

Scobie: Look, we don't have time for this.
The bell will go soon and we need to come
up with some strong arguments showing
that our leaders today *don't* rely on image
more than actions. Okay, let's really
concentrate, work together and focus
on the task at hand.

Kingsley: My sister says Aragorn's hot.

Prindabel: There was a French physicist in the
seventeenth century called Dominique
Arago. I think he worked on
electromagnetism.

Orazio: Why do *we* get the crap side?

Yes, everything seemed to be coming together nicely.

25.
EVERYONE'S ENTITLED TO THEIR OPINION

Somehow, thanks to Scobie, we managed to pull some kind of a case together and scramble to our first debate. Ignatius was first speaker, Orazio was second, Scobie was third and Bill Kingsley (when it was brought to his attention by a dig in the ribs from Razza) was chair. I was the cheer squad. The amazing thing was that we won.

Prindabel knew his speech quite well but delivered it with all the passion of a chemical equation, while every now and then pulling out some obscure fact in a way that was every bit as unexpected and pointless as yanking a rabbit from a hat. Orazio was far less prepared, ad-libbing most of his speech and trusting (wrongly, as it turned out) that his wit and natural charm would gloss over any weaknesses. To say we were ordinary would be generous – we aspired to be ordinary. Fortunately for us, our opposition from Bugner High School made ordinary look stupendous. They reminded me of three guys who'd been dragged off the street and thrown into a police line-up. The only thing that stopped the audience from rising as one and demanding a halt to proceedings on the grounds of unnatural cruelty was the presence of James Scobie.

When Scobie spoke, it was like someone turning on a light in a darkened room. Everything that up until then had been vague and confusing suddenly snapped into focus. You could almost see people rubbing their eyes with the surprise of it all. First Scobie explained the topic (I'm sure that most of the audience had no idea that all the speakers had, in fact, been discussing the same subject). Then he rebuilt the opposition's case from the tangled wreckage they had left in order to systematically and thoroughly dismantle it so that it could never possibly be reassembled. Finally he reviewed our case while at the same time making Prindabel and

Razza seem like learned men. "My second speaker Orazio showed with indisputable logic how…" By the time he had finished there was really no need for an adjudicator's decision.

After that first unexpected victory, the mood in our debating meetings changed. At last we started to get an inkling of what we were trying to do. In the next debate Bill Kingsley replaced Ignatius as first speaker. This was a tactical move by Scobie. We were affirmative for the second debate, and as first affirmative speaker Bill Kingsley wouldn't have to rebut at all. This was crucial, since in our meetings we had discovered that Bill seemed incapable of coming up with a counter-argument of any kind. His response to a possible opposition argument was invariably, "That's quite a good point, actually," or "Everyone's entitled to their opinion."

This time our opposition was St Phoebe's Girls College, and another amazing thing happened – we won again. This was despite Bill Kingsley reading his speech from beginning to end and Razza as chair introducing one of the girls a little too enthusiastically with, "It is my *pleasure* – and I do mean pleasure – to call on the second speaker from St Phoebe's."

Even though we had improved from last time, the difference again was Scobie. It was like having Ian Thorpe swimming the final leg for you in the under sevens floaties relay. As long as we could keep the opposition vaguely in sight, we knew that Scobie would reel them in and eat them up.

Just as he did in the third debate, when, even more amazingly, we defeated Harrison Grammar.

Three wins from three debates automatically put us into the semi-finals. We couldn't believe it. Miss Tarango was ecstatic. We could even afford to lose the next debate and still make it through. We were cruisin'. It was a case of no stress, no pressure, no problems and no worries.

Stay that way?

No chance.

26.
THE BAT CONTROLLER

For a while there I almost felt like I was a normal person. I even started to think that maybe Ishmael Leseur's Syndrome was just a figment of my imagination or that somehow, miraculously, I had been cured. And why wouldn't I? I was a part of the most successful debating team in recent St Daniel's history; James Scobie, school celebrity and personal mascot of the St Daniel's First Fifteen rugby team, was my friend; and Barry Bagsley, my former tormentor, was reduced to a skulking figure in the background. As for Kelly Faulkner... hey, well, who could tell? If I could survive a chronic case of Ishmael Leseur's, anything was possible, right?

Even at home they noticed a change in me. Mum said that I looked like "the cat that got the cream". Dad, on the other hand, said he was worried that too much happiness wasn't character building and suggested that I should think about getting married. This resulted in Mum thumping Dad's shoulder with what he described as "the punch that killed Bruce Lee".

And can you believe this – even Prue was impressed. She called me the brains behind the debating team. That really got me, that one – my little sister Prudence Leseur, official near-genius, saying that *I* was the brains. Talk about the kettle calling the pot an excellent heater of water. Normally it was Prue who stole the limelight. Not that she meant to, or anything like that – she was just being herself. Here, I'll give you a classic example: The Clash of the Peg People.

It all started when I was in Year One at Moorfield Primary and our teacher Miss Sorrensen brought along a box of chunky wooden clothes pegs and said we were going to make some peg people. It was a lot of fun. We drew on faces, gave them cotton wool hair, painted them and made clothes for them.

I made Batman.

I remember spending hours wrapping black tape around the peg to give it muscles, using black crêpe paper for the cape and moulding a headpiece out of black plasticine. When he was finished, I was so proud that I took him out in front to show the whole class. Miss Sorrensen held up my peg Batman and asked, "Who knows who this is?" Nearly every hand shot up straight away. I grinned triumphantly.

"Philip, can you tell us who Ishmael has made?"

"That's easy – the Fat Controller from *Thomas the Tank Engine!*" Philip said confidently, while the rest of the class nodded enthusiastically around him.

Now that would have been bad enough, but the real point of the story is that two years later, when Prue was in Year One, Miss Sorrensen trotted out the peg people idea again. But do you think my little sister Prudence made Batman or Ronald McDonald or even one of the Wiggles? Oh no, she got out Dad's old *Time* magazines, found a series on 'the most influential people of the century', researched around a hundred scientists, thinkers, leaders, artists and entertainers from the past hundred years, and then settled on a top ten consisting of Albert Einstein, Nelson Mandela, Gandhi, Martin Luther

King Jr., Sigmund Freud, the Wright Brothers, John Maynard Keynes, Winston Churchill, Picasso and the Beatles. Then she recreated each of them in peg form with uncanny accuracy and detail. Of course they made my pathetic effort, which Dad had thoughtfully christened the Bat Controller, look like a black blob in comparison.

But the peg people saga didn't stop there. They became an obsession for Prue. Why stop at ten? Why limit them to people from the last one hundred years? What about Shakespeare? Da Vinci? Michelangelo? Newton? Didn't they deserve their own pegs too? Then Mum got into the act. Where are the women? Joan of Arc? Madame Curie? Audrey Hepburn? And what about the writers? Austen? Hemingway? Joyce? Steinbeck? Eliot? Blake? The Brontës? Then Dad hopped on board. Where's Dylan? And Gough. How could you not have Gough?

At last count the peg people numbered more than a hundred, and since Prue insisted that they should be practical as well as educational, I am confronted by them every time it's my turn to peg out the washing. I guess having a little sister who's a near-genius can be a little daunting at times, but it does have its up side. How many people get to choose which of history's most influential, creative and brilliant people will hold up their underpants to dry?

27.
THE OLD BRER RABBIT TRICK

So, like I was saying, for a moment there I almost felt like a normal person. Maybe that was the problem. Maybe I had dropped my guard and left myself open. Whatever the reason, I was about to feel the full effects of Ishmael Leseur's Syndrome.

It all happened on the night of the final preliminary debate. Dad says that one day it will make a good story and that I'll be able to laugh about it. But I've got a feeling that by the time that day arrives I'll be so old I'll probably be laughing every time my teeth fall into my porridge, anyway. Believe me, if there was any way I could avoid writing about this I would, but how else can I explain to you the horror of Ishmael Leseur's?

It all started with a phone call.

"Ishmael? It's Scobie. We've got a bit of a problem."

It was a Wednesday night, about seven o'clock. The debate was on at seven-thirty, and we were up against Lourdes Girls College. Prindabel was unavailable because he was in the school band and they were involved in some competition. (Not surprisingly, he played the triangle.) Our team, therefore, was Kingsley, Razza and Scobie. I was timekeeper, so I didn't need to get there as early as the others.

"Bill Kingsley has laryngitis."

"What?"

"Kingsley has laryngitis. He can't speak – not a word."

I thought back to the meeting we had at lunchtime. Bill hadn't said much, but then again, he never did. There was *something* he said about his throat...

"Ishmael, you still there?"

"I'm here."

"Look, I know I said... well... the thing is... we might need you to fill in... to take Kingsley's place."

I felt like someone had jabbed a hypodermic needle through my chest and pumped a syringe full of liquid nitrogen into my heart. "Why? We're already into the finals. We can just forfeit. It doesn't matter if we lose."

"That would be fine, except there's a 'no forfeit' rule."

"A what?"

"A 'no forfeit' rule – rule 23 of the debating regulations. Any team that forfeits a debate in the preliminary rounds is ineligible to compete in the finals."

I could feel the tone of my voice beginning to slip towards panic. "What sort of a stupid rule is that?"

"It's there to stop teams just not turning up if they qualify early like we did. It's quite reasonable, I think."

Reasonable? I didn't care about what was reasonable. I wanted an escape route. It was time for some frantic straw-clutching. "But what about someone else? There must be someone else who can do it? What about one of the year below us? They're on tonight, as well. We could get one of their reserves. Be a great experience for them. One of them could do it. I can't do it... I'm hopeless... I'm not prepared. Anyway, I've got to do the timekeeping."

"Ishmael, listen. Calm down. *Anyone* can do the timekeeping. Kingsley's here, he can do it – he doesn't need to speak. We can even ask one of the audience if we have to. But we can't ask one of the younger team to take Kingsley's place because they're ineligible. There are only five names on the registration form… and the last one is yours."

"But I'm only the researcher – that's what you said."

"Yes, I know I did." For a moment the line was silent. "Look, Ishmael. I said I'd never *make* you debate and I won't. It's your call entirely. But *this* is the situation. We are one man down. If we can't get a replacement, we have to forfeit. If we forfeit, we are out of the finals. The simple fact is that *you* are the only one who can take Bill Kingsley's place. There is no one else."

Great. No pressure. This would be easy. All I had to say was, "Sorry, love to help out, but I think I'll give it miss. Shame about those finals and letting the team and the school and Miss Tarango and everyone else down – after all that hard work too. But as you say, it's my call entirely, so if it's all the same with you, I'd rather not."

I don't, of course. I cling pathetically to one last feeble strand of straw as I sink blue and bloated into the watery depths. "But I'll be hopeless…"

"You'll be fine. After all, you practically wrote Bill Kingsley's speech for him, and you have a far better understanding of the topic and our case than he ever did. Just read it out. And look, even if you don't do so well, what does it matter? Win or lose, we still get through to the finals... and we'll have you to thank for it."

I could hear James Scobie breathing on the other end of the line. I imagined his mouth twisting as he waited for my reply and I thought of all the times he had put himself in the firing line – standing up to Barry Bagsley, facing up to the school assembly, taking on the might of Churchill Grammar, dragging our team of struggling first-time debaters across the finish line time after time. Yet James 'No Fear' Scobie had it easy, didn't he? I really couldn't tell you why I asked the next question, although I have often wondered about it. Perhaps being on the phone with just a voice between me and the answer made it easier somehow.

"Scobie... you know that story... about the tumour and the operation and everything... and about never being afraid? Is it really true?"

A long silence followed. I pictured Scobie's face frozen mid-twist. Finally I heard his voice. It seemed different somehow.

"Sort of... the tumour, the operation... they're true.

The other thing… not being afraid… well, it depends on how you look at it. Maybe it wasn't a scalpel that did it. Maybe… when you're lying in an operating theatre and someone is cutting into your brain… and you don't know whether you're going to…"

For a few seconds all I could hear was Scobie breathing. When he continued it was almost in a whisper.

"Well… maybe there's just so much fear you can have… and in that one moment you use up all the fear you were ever supposed to feel… and it's the fear that cuts you… and it cuts you so deep that you just decide that nothing else is worth being afraid of… and that nothing is going to scare you any more… because you just won't let it."

I didn't know what to say. The image of Barry Bagsley towering over James Scobie and counting to five with his clenched fist poised to strike leaped into my mind. Then it was quickly replaced by a pale boy with a spider wrapped around his face like a hand.

"But what about the bugs and spiders and stuff? How…?"

"My father is an entomologist," Scobie said calmly. "He studies bugs and spiders and stuff. I grew up with bugs and spiders and stuff. Some kids had rattles and squeaky toys in their cots. I had tarantulas and beetles. What happened in class was just the old Brer Rabbit trick. The Barry Bagsleys of this world can't resist throwing you into the briar patch."

Before I could ask Scobie exactly what he was talking about he cut back in.

"Ishmael. We really don't have much time here. The debate starts in 15 minutes. According to the rules we've only got 10 minutes after that, then it's officially a forfeit. If you don't leave almost straight away you won't make it. You need to decide now. Can I tell them you're coming?"

As much as I wished it wasn't true, I knew there was only one possible answer to that question. "Yes... I'll be there." And that was it. I hung up the phone and checked my watch. Scobie was right. It was going to be close. There wasn't even time to think about the other question I had wanted to ask him – about whether that last part of his story was true or not.

You know, the bit about him being fine and the tumour being gone.

28.
DEAD MAN
WALKING

"Mum? Where's all my school stuff gone? I can't find any of my clothes. Mum? I need a clean school uniform. Mum? Mum!"

Panic and hysteria were arm-wrestling inside me. Someone had taken all my school gear. I'd have to debate in my boxers. But why would someone steal all my school gear? This couldn't be happening. Wait, maybe it really wasn't happening. Maybe I was just having one of those crazy dreams where you turn up somewhere in your pyjamas or with no pants on. Of course! That was it! It was all just a dream. I was only dreaming! None of it was true. I didn't have to debate at all. It wasn't real.

How could it be? What an idiot I was. Entire school uniforms don't just disappear without explanation.

"I washed yesterday. Have you checked the line?"

Oh… right.

I sprinted downstairs and out to the garden. I madly grabbed my shirt, shorts and socks, wrenching them from the line and sending a half-dozen or so of the world's most influential people cartwheeling to earth. Sorry, Prue. I checked my watch. Twenty past seven – oh my god – time for warp speed. I charged back to my room, tore off my clothes and blasted on some sickly-smelling deodorant.

"That shirt will need ironing," Mum called.

"Haven't got time – I'll wear my jumper."

I quickly attacked my school uniform, flung on my shirt, strangled the buttons and yanked up my shorts. Hardly pausing for breath, I wrestled on my jumper, jerked up my socks, stomped on my shoes, snatched up a fistful of pens, jammed them in my pocket, ripped a comb through my hair, shouted goodbye, tore through the house, jumped in the car and lashed on the seatbelt.

"You okay?" Dad asked.

"Yeah." (Except that every meal I had ever eaten

was on the verge of making an encore appearance.)

"Sure?"

"Yeah." (If you ignore the fact that some alien beast was growing inside me and was just waiting for the most appropriate time to burst through my chest.)

"Feeling worried?"

"A bit." (Yeah, that bit where my entire nervous system had gone into meltdown and was leaking into my shoes.)

"Well, we're all proud of you. You'll be fine. Just stay positive and try not to worry."

"Okay." (No problem. I'd sailed past 'worry' three or four levels of hysteria ago.)

The rest of the journey was a blur. Apart from feeling the pens in my pocket jabbing into my leg, I was numb with dread.

"Here we are, and 5 minutes to spare. Sure you don't want me to come up for moral support?"

"No, I'll be okay." (There were some things a father shouldn't have to see.)

"Okay."

"Thanks for the lift."

"No problem," Dad said, glancing quickly around as

if he were afraid of being overheard. "Old jungle saying: Sometimes the Phantom travels the streets as a normal man… this is one of those nights."

For Dad's sake I forced a smile. "Well, you don't have to worry about picking me up – I'm getting a lift with Mrs Zorzotto."

"Okay, I'll see you then… And look, mate… just do your best, all right? You'll be fine. Remember, stay positive."

"Thanks, Dad."

"Right, then – my work here is done. Back to the Skull Cave."

I watched my father drive off into the night. We had a lot in common. He was 'The Ghost Who Walks' and I was a dead man walking. I tried to push that thought from my mind as I headed upstairs to the debating room.

Scobie was waiting at the door to usher me quickly to my seat. I knew every eye would be on me, and so as we came in I showed intense interest in the pattern and design of the floor tiles. We managed to make it to our desks, which were on the far side of the room, angled slightly to face the audience. I sat down between Scobie and Razza and pulled a stack of blank index cards from my shirt pocket. I stared at them as if they had the answers to the greatest mysteries of the universe carved on them. My face was burning like a flare.

Scobie handed me Bill Kingsley's index cards, the ones I had helped to write over the last couple of days. Then he gave me what I interpreted as an encouraging smile but what in fact looked more like the demented leer of a homicidal maniac.

I turned to look at Razza. He was scribbling something on an index card. He slid it across to me. I picked it up. It had a stick figure drawn on it with its arms thrown into the air. A giant arrow was sticking out of its chest. Above the drawing was the word 'Twang!' in capital letters. I frowned and looked back at him. His face was one sickly smirk. He raised his eyebrows and nodded towards the other side of the room.

I lifted my head for the first time. The girls from Lourdes College sat opposite us. They were huddled together whispering intently. One of them glanced up. My heart froze. I was staring into the ice-blue eyes of Kelly Faulkner. Razza pushed another card my way. I snaffled it up and nodded my head thoughtfully while I read it so that Kelly Faulkner would think it contained some deep philosophical debating point. All it said was 'Hubba hubba!'

A scraping chair startled me back to reality. The Lourdes girl who was chairing the debate stood up. She was behind the desk that separated the two teams. Beside her was Bill Kingsley. He was holding a stopwatch and gazing palely into deep space.

"Ladies and Gentlemen, welcome to this fourth-round debate between St Daniel's College Moorfield and Lourdes College Hillview. The topic for tonight's debate is: *That the private lives of public figures should remain private.* Our adjudicator tonight is…"

As the chairperson droned on I peeked around the classroom. There were about fifteen or so people in the audience. Miss Tarango wasn't there because she was with one of the other teams. Mrs Zorzotto was there, along with Bill Kingsley's father and little sister. Down the back was the adjudicator – a young girl with spiky red hair. The rest were Lourdes supporters.

I lowered my eyes to the empty space between the two teams and tried to imagine myself walking out there to speak. Suddenly my legs began to jump and shake and I had to grab them and hold them down like I was wrestling two baby crocodiles. Then my stomach started slurping and churning like a dying washing machine. I felt like I was about to pass out. I had to pull myself together.

What was it that Dad said? Stay positive. All right. It was time to fill my mind with positive thoughts. Let's see, positive thought number one – in about 10 minutes it would all be over. Good! Positive thought number two – whatever happened, it wasn't going to kill me. That's true! Positive thought number three – a lot of people had to face much worse things like war, persecution, poverty or watching reality TV, so why should I worry about a silly debate? I shouldn't!

Hey, this positive thinking trick was actually working. Maybe it wouldn't be as bad as I thought. After all, what was the worst that could happen? Well, let's see… the worst… the worst would have to be if I went totally blank and turned into a bumbling, stuttering, gibbering, dribbling, babbling, um-ing and ah-ing baboon, then had to stand there like a shop dummy until I was stripped of every last shred of dignity and ended up having the self-worth of an amoeba.

Looking back, I really wish it had gone that well.

29.
DEAD TO THE
POWER DEAD

"Ladies and Gentlemen, to open the debate I call on the first speaker for the Affirmative, Kelly Faulkner, to commence her team's case."

Kelly Faulkner stood up, walked briskly to the front of the room, took a breath, looked up and smiled. For some reason my heart decided at that moment that it could afford to skip a couple of beats before thudding back to life with a mega jolt.

"Twang!" Razza whispered from the corner of his mouth.

I rolled my eyes and ignored him. I had no time for his childishness. This was a serious business. I had to focus all my energy on analysing, dissecting and refuting the opposition's argument. I held my pen poised over a blank sheet of paper and waited.

"Ladies and gentlemen, madam chair," Kelly Faulkner began calmly, "imagine the following scenario. A politician dedicates her life to serving her community. She devotes her time to helping…"

What was it about her voice? It sounded like… like… I don't know… like something happy… something warm… and friendly and close… like a secret… or a Christmas present or something. And those eyes… how do you make your eyes do that? How do you make your eyes smile? My eyes just sit there like a couple of dead bugs. And look at the little bulges of her cheeks… Hey, wait a minute! What was I doing? I was supposed to be listening, you know, so I could analyse, dissect, and refute.

"… and that is our theme for tonight's debate."

Theme? What theme? I didn't hear anything about a theme. Oh my god, I've missed the theme! I looked at Scobie. He was writing vigorously on an index card. Thank god. At least Scobie had nailed the theme. When he had finished he stabbed a full stop and shot the note across to me with a knowing nod. I looked at the card.

There was a word at the top underlined by two heavy pen strokes. That is, I was pretty sure it was a word. With Scobie's loopy, slanted writing it could have been a doodle or even a decorative border for all I knew. I was guessing and hoping that it said 'Theme'.

Underneath that heading were three lines of writing. They looked like rows of flattened bowling pins. I held the card closer to my eyes. I rotated and twisted it to every conceivable angle. I thought I recognised the word 'bubblegum'. I turned back to Scobie. He smiled knowingly. I smiled back haven't-got-a-clue-ingly. This was bad. I had no idea what their theme was. I decided to just forget it. The crucial thing was to get down the main points of their argument for rebuttal.

I turned my attention back to Kelly Faulkner.

She flicked over an index card. God, she had cute hands. I wondered what it would be like to hold one, to feel those soft little fingers. And look at her nails – they were so clean and neat, not like mine, which looked like they'd been cut with a chainsaw. And her hair – all shiny and held back with those little clips. The more I watched her the more I realised that everything about her was just so neat and cute and...

"... Now for my second point."

Second point! What happened to the first point? And what about the team outline? How could I have missed the entire outline of the Affirmative case? Okay. Don't panic. Just get the second point. At least I'd have one thing to rebut.

"My second point is that privacy is a basic human right. Surely public figures are entitled to the same rights as everyone else. Just because someone is well known it doesn't make him or her public property. For example..."

Yeah... that's not a bad point, actually. After all, everyone's got to have some privacy, right? I mean, even if you are a public figure like a film star or a politician, what gives other people the right to think that they should be allowed to know... Hold on! What am I doing? I can't *agree* with her. There has to be a counter argument. Think... think... *Think*!

Clunk!

Bill Kingsley had attempted to ring the three-minute warning bell but had only succeeded in smothering it with his big mitt. A minute to go! I had to come up with something fast. Wait, what about the Four Steps of Effective Rebuttal? I was desperate. It was worth a shot. Let's see, the opposition says that privacy is a basic human right. They are wrong because… because… because…

"… so in conclusion…"

In *conclusion*! No, it can't be. I'm not ready!

"… the private lives of public figures should remain private because people in the public eye are still living and breathing people – not public property."

The audience applauded enthusiastically. Kelly Faulkner sat down. Her teammates huddled in, whispering and smiling. One of them squeezed her hand. I wondered what that would feel… no, forget about it… I needed to think… I needed to calm down… I needed help! Just then Scobie pushed a stack of index cards my way. I desperately flicked through them. More rows and rows of scuttled bowling pins. Wait! Was that the letter T? Or maybe a Q? And there, was that something about a woollen balloon? Or possibly… but it was hopeless. I was just kidding myself. I was doomed. There was nowhere else to turn. Or was there?

Razza tapped me on the shoulder. He held out a card. All right! The Big Z had obviously used his superior knowledge of the Four Steps of Effective Rebuttal to blow the opposition's case apart. The Razzman to the rescue! I snatched the card and hungrily devoured his pearl of wisdom.

'Your girlfriend's got *hot* legs!'

Orazio nudged me in the ribs, pushed out his lips and pretended to fan his face with his hand. I was dead. I was deader than dead. There were five-thousand-year-old mummies that weren't as dead as me. I was dead to the power dead. I had no time left. The adjudicator had stopped writing and was trying to catch the eye of the chairperson. I was next up. Quickly I bundled up the blank index cards with the useless ones Razza and Scobie had given me and pushed them aside. The chairperson began to stand. I squirmed in my seat. Something hard dug uncomfortably into my groin. I shoved my hands into my pockets looking for what I assumed was a missing pen, but my pockets were empty. What the…?

"And now to open his team's case I call on…"

I felt around the front of my shorts. There seemed to be something *in* my pants and it wasn't part of me!

"… the first speaker for the Negative team… ah…"

Oh no. The Lourdes girl had squeezed her face into a prune and was squinting at her notes.

"...Itch... meal... Les... soooer?" she said, like she was gagging on a chicken bone. Thanks again, Dad.

I snatched up my index cards, fought with my chair and tripped my way to the front of the audience. When I got there, I told myself to relax, to breathe deeply, but my legs were performing some kind of wild tribal dance and the rest of my body seemed to be going into spasm. I clenched my index cards and held on for dear life.

4 minutes, I told myself. 4 minutes and it would all be over.

Little did I know.

30.
BLANKING HELL!

It was now or never. I knew the first sentence of the speech off by heart. I looked the audience right in the space a metre or so above their eyes. My legs were jumping like crazy. I took a deep breath. I just hoped that when I opened my mouth something vaguely approaching recognisable words would come out.

"Ladies and gentlemen, madam chair..." Not bad, apart from sounding like I was being strangled by one of those vibrating exercise belts. "Tonight my team will prove to you that..." Now be careful here. Don't mess it up. "... that the public part of private lives... um... the public lives of private people... wait... public figures on private property… ahhh… the private part of public property… the public… the private…" Oh my god. The topic had turned to chop suey in my mind. I had to concentrate – get it right and get it out. Okay, here goes. "… that the private parts of public figures should be made public."

There, at last… wait on… what was that murmuring, snuffling noise? I risked a quick glance around the room. What were the audience grinning about? Why did the spiky-haired adjudicator have her mouth open? Why was that Lourdes girl choking on her water? Why was Razza lying on the desk shaking? Why was Scobie's face screwed up like a rag? What was the matter with these people? Didn't they understand that debating was a serious business?

I had no time to solve this mystery. Best just to keep going. I shifted my legs to try to stop my kneecaps from leaping off. I felt another soft jab high up in my inner thigh. What was that? Either there was a part of me that I didn't know about or some foreign object had made a home for itself in my pants. I slid my right hand down and lightly fingered the front of my shorts. I glanced up. Everyone's eyes were locked on my groin. I snapped my hand back to my index card. I felt like someone had shoved my head in an oven and twirled the dial to roast. Say something, say something... say *something*!

"Ahhh... ummm... ahhh..." Now I was burning up. "... before I... ah... continue with my team's case... ah... I would like to rebut... a couple of points made by the first speaker from the Affirmative team." Yes, I definitely would have liked to, but unfortunately I didn't have a clue how to! It didn't stop me, however, from launching blindly into the Four Steps of Effective Rebuttal.

"She said that privacy was a basic human right. This is not true because... because..." *Come on, Four Steps of Effective Rebuttal, don't desert me now.* "... because... if everyone had privacy... people in the magazine industry would be out of a job." *What? Doesn't matter – keep going.* "We say if you want privacy, then don't become a public figure." Okay, I know, not exactly brilliant, but who cares? I was home and hosed. Now it was straight to the index cards, head down and start reading.

I looked at the first card. I saw three rows of flattened bowling pins. I flicked over to the second – more flattened bowling pins. I frantically shuffled to the third... the fourth... the fifth – an entire bowling alley of flattened bowling pins flashed before my eyes! Somehow I must have got Scobie's notes mixed up with Kingsley's. I turned over another card. Surely here I would find something intelligible. The words 'Hubba hubba!' leered back at me. I told myself not to panic. Fortunately the next card was very helpful. Let's see, my first point would be that the private lives of public figures should be made public because... my girlfriend has hot legs. Yes, that would work juuuust fine. I began to shuffle through the remaining cards with skyrocketing desperation. The next card was blank. The next one... blank. Then... blank... blank, blank, blank, blank, blank, blank, blank. *Blanking hell!*

I looked back to my desk. Bill Kingsley's index cards were on the floor under my chair. Would the adjudicator take off points if I crawled under the desk to get them? I glanced up. Everyone was watching me and waiting. My head-oven turned itself up to 'scorch' and my legs started doing a Riverdance. But not only that, something else was happening. Whatever had taken up residence in my pants was working loose. I could feel it slipping.

I tried to keep still, but I was so nervous my hips

were shaking like a hula dancer's. The thing in my shorts dropped down another notch. I twisted my right leg in and up to stop it. I looked like I was busting to go to the loo. I fumbled with my palm cards. The 'thing' slid lower down my thigh. It was hard and cigar-shaped. I twisted my leg further around till I was balancing on one foot. But it was no use. Whatever was down there was dropping... dropping... dropping... At the last moment I made a desperate lunge and clamped my hand on my shorts. But I was too late. A blurred object shot from my boxers, bounced off the toe of my shoe and skidded across the tiles. It pulled up about 2 metres in front of me, spinning like a dying propeller.

I held my breath.

The spinning stopped. So did my heart.

From vast experience with such matters I can tell you that there are certain times in your life when it's best to pretend that something that obviously just happened, didn't.

"For my first point..." I said, holding up my left index finger in a feeble attempt at a gesture.

But no one was listening. They weren't even looking at me. Every eye in the room was fixed on the old wooden clothes peg that lay on the floor. It had a big nose and a mop of dark hair.

I abandoned my first point and joined in the communal stare.

One of the Beatles had just fallen out of my pants.

I was pretty sure it was Ringo.

31.
TIME FOR
BEDDY-BYES

The next thing I knew, Prue's peg person was being swallowed by darkness. I tried to lift my head but my neck had turned to rubber and my legs seemed to have decided that it was time for beddy-byes. Then the whole room turned into a jumping castle and the last thing I saw before I passed out completely was Kelly Faulkner's face rushing towards me.

When I came to, cold and clammy, in another room, all I remember is people fussing over me and asking me if I was all right and my brain working in slow motion so that if I turned my head too quickly everything blurred then sloshed to a halt and left me dizzy.

After that there was the drive home with Razza babbling on until his mum finally said, "Orazio Zorzotto, for once in your life, shut up!" When we got to my place Mrs Zorzotto said she'd explain everything to my parents, and so I went straight to my room.

Of course Mum and Dad came up later and told me not to worry about what had happened and that I had been brave and that they were proud of me. Dad also added that if anyone was going to fall from your pants it might as well be a Beatle because the Beatles were the best group there ever was. He did make the point, however, that if he had his choice he would have picked John, Paul or George to drop from his trousers because Ringo was by far the least talented. Even better still, he suggested that if there was room in my pants it would have been great to have a Fab Four reunion. I think my father might have been trying to lighten the mood. It didn't work.

Then Prue came in and said she was sorry one of her peg people had caused so much trouble, but she suggested that the probability of something like that happening would be astronomical and that I should feel privileged to have been part of such a mathematically improbable chain of events. I didn't. When she heard what Dad said about the Beatles she said it would have been better if it had been the Sigmund Freud peg that had fallen from my pants because of the 'sexual connotations' and because then the whole incident could be dismissed as a 'Freudian slip'. I wasn't sure what all that meant, so we just looked at each other for a couple of seconds and then she left.

When I went to bed that night, I was hoping that I would wake up and find that it was all a dream. (Even though Miss Tarango wouldn't have liked this, because she told us that if anyone in the class ever gave her an essay that ended with 'it was all just a dream!' she would rip it up, bake it into a pie and make us eat it.)

Of course, when I woke up it wasn't a dream. Miss Tarango would be happy at least, but I was left feeling like a blob of that grey gunk that Dad scrapes out from our kitchen plughole.

32.
CLOSE ENCOUNTER
OF THE NERD KIND

"Tell me again why you had a little wooden dolly shoved up your pants."

It was the next day – Thursday lunchtime – and we were having our usual debriefing session.

"It wasn't a doll," I said wearily in reply to Razza's never-ending questions, "it was one of my sister's peg people. I told you, it must have got caught on my pants or my shirt or something when I pulled my clothes from the line. I was in a hurry. I didn't have time to think. I just… I didn't…" I gave up.

"Peg people?"

"It's a long story," I said darkly.

"All right," Scobie interrupted, "I think it would be more beneficial if we just got on with the debriefing."

"Shouldn't take long."

"Thank you, Orazio. Now, if we could start?" Scobie said coldly.

Razza was right, though. What was there to debrief? Following my stunning performance the debate was stopped and the points were awarded to Lourdes College.

"Now obviously, there's not much we can say about the actual debate itself…"

"Oh, I don't know. I reckon Leseur's dive was worth at least nine out of ten – bit too much of a splash on entry for a perfect score. Still, I think…" Razza finally wilted under Scobie's glare.

"As I was saying… the purpose of this meeting is to thank Ishmael. Things may not have gone *exactly* to plan last night, but if it wasn't for Ishmael stepping in at the last moment, we would have been out of the finals. So I think we should all give him a round of applause."

Scobie, Prindabel and Bill Kingsley clapped while Razza whistled, pounded on the desk and made a sound with his mouth like a roaring crowd.

"Yeah, I got to admit, Ishmael, you came through,

man – the cavalry to the rescue. But I reckon they'll have to rewrite the debating handbook. Why worry about preparing a case or trying to rebut the other team's argument? Just practise the Leseur Lunge. Yeah, when all else fails, grope one of the opposition."

"What?"

Razza stopped and stared at me.

Scobie, Bill and Prindabel stared at me.

"What do you mean, 'grope one of the opposition'?"

Razza turned to Scobie. "Oh my god, I don't think he knows."

Scobie frowned and shifted uncomfortably in his seat. "Ishmael, do you remember what you were doing just before you... passed out?"

"Yes. Trying not to pass out."

"Do you remember anything after that?"

"No. I was passed out," I said, becoming more irritated with the pointless questions.

"Well, yes," Scobie said with a bleak smile, "but for instance, do you recall making a gesture with your left hand?"

"Yeah... so what?"

"Well..."

"Let me tell him. I'll tell him. Come on. Please. I'll do it."

Something about Razza's enthusiasm was deeply disturbing.

"No. I think it would be better coming from me."

That didn't sound good. That was the kind of line people said in soap operas when they were about to deliver some devastating news like, "I'm leaving you, Rodney. I'm marrying your evil twin brother who everyone thought died in that explosion but who really escaped and had plastic surgery and for the last ten years has been our gardener and... my *lover!*"

Scobie faced me and frowned. "After you made that gesture with your left hand – which, incidentally, was a very good attempt at a non-oral persuasive technique..."

"Quit stalling, Scobie," Razza said impatiently.

"After that... you started to fall forward... and then I guess because your arm was up... you overbalanced to the left... and then you obviously tried to break your fall because you reached out..." Scobie hesitated before adding, "and that's when your left hand... came in *contact*... with the opposition – or, more particularly, the first speaker of the opposition."

"Yeah, she had sort of a close encounter of the *nerd* kind," Razza said.

"Oh god. She's all right, isn't she? I didn't hurt her, did I?"

James Scobie stared back vacantly.

"Well, did I?"

Razza looked around at the others, beaming like a lighthouse. Prindabel's thin lips were pressed into a grin, as if he had just received the latest edition of *Algebra Monthly*. Even Bill Kingsley stopped drinking from a big carton of strawberry milk long enough for a brief flicker of something close to comprehension to scuttle across his face. This was bad. This was very bad. There was only one possible subject where those three could find common ground.

"Scobie, what *kind* of... contact?" I asked with growing dread. "Scobie? What kind of contact did I make with Kelly... with the first speaker of the opposition?"

Scobie opened his mouth to speak, but before he had the chance Razza leaped from his chair, placed his hand on my shoulder and leaned in close. "Let's just say, Ishy you old devil..." and suddenly Razza's hand had slipped down to my chest. "… it looked like you were very keen to keep a-*breast* of the opposition's argument."

"What?" I said, flinging Razza's hand away.

"Don't worry, she probably just thought you were rebutting one of her impressive *points*."

"What?!" I reeled around in horror. "Scobie, what's he on about?"

By now Razza was prancing around the room like a prizefighter, digging Prindabel in the ribs and slapping Bill Kingsley on the back.

"It wasn't your fault. It obviously wasn't intentional," Scobie said reasonably. "It's just… she was there… and your hand was reaching out. No one thinks for a minute that you…"

"Oh my god!" I looked from Scobie to the other three grinning faces. "Oh my god! No! You're making it up. You're lying. It's rubbish."

"Ishmael my man, calm down. It's no big deal. She'll understand. Just tell her that you're a *hands on* sort of a guy."

"Oh my god. That's it. My life is over. Just take me out and shoot me."

Razza bobbed in again. "Look, Ishmael, I don't know

why you're so upset. I think what you did was very brave."

"Brave? What the hell are you talking about!"

"Well, who knows, she could have been *booby*-trapped." Razza whooped and bounced around, pushing and prodding Prindabel and Bill Kingsley. "Eh, eh, booby-trapped?... doncha see?... *booby*?... *boob*?"

"Orazio, could you be serious for a minute? Ishmael's obviously upset and you're not helping."

"Sorry, sorry," Razza said, lowering his head and holding up his hands as if to deflect Scobie's glare, "but I really think he's making too big a deal out of it. As far as I'm concerned that chick just got a bit of her own medicine back."

"What?" This time it was Scobie's turn to be confused. "What do you mean, her own medicine?"

"Well she had a bit of a go at us in her speech, didn't she? So Ishmael had a go at her – sort of like *tit* for tat."

This time Razza draped himself between Prindabel and Bill Kingsley, wrapped his arms around their necks and pulled them in. "*Tit* for tat! *Tit* for tat! Somebody stop me!"

Ignatius Prindabel's face contorted in a bizarre leer until he looked like Mr Burns from *The Simpsons*, and his head bobbed up and down and air hissed in and out between his teeth. At the same time Bill Kingsley began to make a strange noise like an engine struggling to turn over. "Errummm… errumm… errummm."

Not only had I shown Kelly Faulkner that I was a babbling idiot as well as a deviate who liked to store wooden objects in his pants and a wimp who passed out under pressure, I could now add 'pervert' to my impressive list of credentials. There was only one course of action left open to me. I wrapped my arms around my head, lay on the desk and moaned.

"Look, Ishmael…"

"Orazio, that's enough!"

"Scobes, I'm just trying to *help* here. Give me *some* credit, will you? I think I know where to draw the line. Okay? As I was saying… look, Ishmael, I know you think that that Kelly chick is perfect, like some sort of a goddess or angel or something, but are you sure you're not getting carried away?"

"What's your point exactly, Zorzotto?" I mumbled from under my arms, sensing danger.

"My point is, Ishmael, that maybe not everyone thinks she's perfect. What I'm trying to say is, I'm sure she's got her *knockers*. But hey, I don't have to tell *you* that, do I?"

At this point Razza collapsed on the floor holding his stomach and groaning with laughter. Meanwhile Prindabel hissed and spluttered with even greater intensity and Bill Kingsley's grinding engine noise seemed on the verge of lurching into life. It was only Scobie's hard, unwavering voice that sliced through the simmering hysteria.

"Orazio, show a bit of maturity for once. We're here to support Ishmael. So let's cut out all this nonsense over what are, after all, just mammary glands."

"Just what?" Razza managed to choke out while he gasped for air.

"Mammary glands," Scobie replied like a dictionary, "the milk-producing gland in female mammals. In other mammals called the udder but in humans called the breast."

Razza dragged himself to his feet. "You're a sick individual, do you know that, Scobie?" he said seriously. "It's people like you that give us perverts a bad name."

I lifted my head from the desk. There was only one question I wanted answered. "What will I say to her?"

Four pairs of eyes turned towards me.

"Kelly Faulkner – what will I say to her?"

I looked around for an answer. Prindabel and Bill Kingsley stared back like pre-schoolers asked to explain the scientific theory behind the existence of black holes. Even Razza had run out of smart replies and weak puns. Scobie was my last hope. Scobie always knew what to say. He could always find the right words.

"Scobie? If I ever see Kelly Faulkner again, what could I possibly say to her?" I asked hopelessly.

Scobie pushed his lips to a pout, wrinkled his brow and put his mouth through the full range of twists and stretches. "Well... I think you have to try to see the big picture. This could turn out to be one of those interesting stories people tell about how they first met. So perhaps you could say..." Scobie stopped and his eyes flicked towards Razza.

"What? What could I say?"

"... thanks for the *mammary*?"

33.
THE REALLY UGLY PART

What followed wasn't pretty. Scobie's joke finally kickstarted Bill Kingsley's motor. Unfortunately he had just filled his mouth with strawberry milk and he immediately began to moan and buck like a cow giving birth. Razza, in turn, let out strangled cries like he was being stabbed and leaped about pointing at Scobie and Kingsley and shaking his head in disbelief. Prindabel, meanwhile, began shaking like a boiling kettle and making high-pitched humming noises, as if he were trying to keep a swarm of bees inside his mouth. Scobie just twisted his face into a knot and tried to look innocent.

The really ugly part came when strawberry milk

bubbled out of Bill Kingsley's nose like pink lava and Ignatius Prindabel, under the immense strain of keeping everything inside, broke wind like a trumpet hitting three octaves above high C. This caused Razza to bolt from the room wiping tears from his eyes with one hand and clutching at his groin with the other. He was followed closely by Bill Kingsley sputtering like a pink fountain and Ignatius Prindabel tooting like a brass band. It was quite a parade.

Needless to say, I was overwhelmed by how supportively my friends had rallied around in my time of personal crisis.

Only Scobie remained in the classroom, smiling sheepishly back at me.

"I'm a complete loser."

"I don't think so. You showed the true St Daniel's spirit last night – you entered the lion's den."

"Yeah, and fainted," I said glumly.

"But not before you stood up."

"What difference does that make?"

"Well, it's like what Miss Tarango's been saying about the short stories we're writing – about not going on too long and knowing when to end them? Well, I think your story ended when you got up in front of that audience. That's all we really needed to know about you."

At home that night I tried desperately to erase the whole Kelly Faulkner groping disaster from my mind. But it wasn't that easy to just edit out all the excruciatingly embarrassing chunks of your life like they never existed. Maybe Razza had the right approach. Maybe I was taking it all too seriously. Maybe it was best to just laugh about it and try to put things into perspective. After all, I still had my family and I still had my friends (even though their sense of humour left a lot to be desired) and my life was still relatively Barry Bagsley-free.

Yes, when I looked at the big picture, I realised that things could definitely be worse for me – a lot worse, in fact.

And before I knew it, they were.

34.
DROWNING IN OUR OWN OFFAL

It was on the first day after the holidays that we heard the news.

"What do mean, he won't be back for the finals?"

"Look, Ignatius, I'm just telling you what Miss Tarango told me. Scobie's with his father in Sydney for some reason and he won't be back in time for the finals."

"But he *is* coming back, right?" Razza asked.

"Sure, yeah, of course." But the trouble was, I wasn't that certain.

When I asked Miss Tarango the same question all she said was, "As far as I know," and for a moment there she seemed to have lost her dimples.

"Without Scobie we're dead."

"That's the spirit, Prindabel. Need any help hoisting the white flag?"

"Well, I suppose that *you're* going to take Scobie's place are you, Orazio?"

"No, but at least I'm not throwing in the towel before I even know the topic."

"Ahhh…" This was going to be delicate. "That's another thing Miss Tarango told me. For the semi-final rounds… it's a secret topic."

"What? Secret topic? How will we know what we have to talk about?"

"I've got a hunch, Billy Boy," Razza said, putting his arm around Bill Kingsley and speaking like a kindergarten teacher, "that maybe, just maybe, if we're extra specially good and eat up all our vegetables, they might let us in on the secret *before* we actually start debating. Would I be right, Ishmael?"

"Right. We get the topic on the night. Then they lock us in a room with some encyclopedias and a dictionary. We can't talk to anyone outside. We've only got an hour to prepare."

"An *hour*?" Razza said in disbelief. "Last debate

it took us an entire *week* just to explain the *topic* to Kingsley."

"Now do you want to hear the really bad news? Our opposition is Preston College."

The looks on their faces said it all. If you went to Preston College and didn't become at least prime minister you were considered a disappointment. At Preston College they started debating in the womb. We were certainly up against it. The trick was to remain positive.

"They're going to kill us. They're going to chew us up, spit us out and grind us into the dirt. They're going to massacre us. It'll be a blood bath. We'll be ripped to shreds and torn apart. We'll be drowning in our own offal."

"Tell me, Prindabel, have you ever thought of a career as a motivational speaker?"

"And Orazio, I suppose *you* think we can *actually* win?"

"*Actually* I don't. That's about as likely as Kingsley here outrunning a three-toed sloth, *but* at least I'm willing to *pretend* that we can win."

"Well, I'm not. Why kid ourselves? I think we should forfeit. We're down to four already. If a couple of us say we're sick, what can they do? Look, we made the finals, didn't we? We've done better than anyone expected. If we're going to lose anyway, what does it matter? Orazio might want to make a fool of himself, but what about the rest of you? Kingsley, what do you say?"

"I don't mind."

"That's the way, Billy Boy!" Razza said, punching him on the shoulder. "What's one more humiliation after a lifetime, eh? What about you, Ishmael?"

"That's not fair. What's he care? He doesn't have to get up there while those cyborgs from Preston cut us to ribbons."

Prindabel was right. I couldn't really say whether we should debate or not unless I was willing to be part of it. I thought long and hard before I replied.

"I don't think we should forfeit. I think we owe it to Scobie to at least try."

Prindabel looked wildly around the room. "Is anybody listening here? Hello, can anybody hear me? We haven't got a hope – I repeat, not a hope."

"Neither did Peter Chung when he took on the Mighty Cro-Magnon."

"Ishmael's right," Razza said. "Don't give up! Don't give in!"

"Well, I think you're all mad."

"Look, Prindabel, we really need you there on the night. We need all that stuff you've got in your head – all those facts and figures." I had to brace myself before I could go on. "Look, I'll make a deal with you. If you don't want to speak on the night... if you don't want to do it... then I'll take your place. Just as long as you're there to help us out with our case. Okay?"

"Okay... Yeah, that's fine by me... I'll be there."

So it was done. I didn't know whether to feel relieved or depressed. I guess it's the sort of feeling you'd expect when you'd just succeeded in driving the last nail in your own coffin.

35.
DEATH BY LETHAL INJECTION

Two weeks later we were locked in a classroom at Preston College. I looked out the window. It was three floors down to a hard concrete playground. I'd almost convinced myself that I could survive the jump when the door clicked open.

One of the adjudicators stood in the doorway holding a folded slip of paper. As I was closest, I took it from him and brought it to the table where the others were waiting. Prindabel was pale. Bill Kingsley was disturbingly calm. Orazio was as jumpy and as pumped as the Duracell Bunny.

"Here goes nothing," I said opening the paper,

half-expecting to see the words *Death by Lethal Injection.*

"Well? What is it? What's the topic?" they all chorused.

"The topic is, *That science fiction and fantasy films have little relevance to the problems facing today's world.*"

After a few seconds of silence and quickly exchanged glances, Prindabel was the first to speak. "Well that's not too bad," he said slowly with a flicker of hope in his eye. "You know, when you think of actual problems in the world... stuff like AIDS, pollution, global warming... drugs... well, what do films like *Spiderman* or *Lord of the Rings* or *Harry Potter* or *Star Wars* have to say about those?"

Prindabel's eyes began to flash madly about as if he were seeing ideas leap around inside his head. "Yeah... Hey, I know... we can even argue that science fiction and fantasy movies are just escapes... you know, that they just *distract* us from facing *real* problems... Hey, that could be part of our theme!" Prindabel snatched up a pen and began writing feverishly. "Look... we can do this... those films are totally irrelevant to world problems... here, these could be our three main arguments... first we could say that..."

"Ignatius. We're *Negative*. We have to argue that science fiction and fantasy films are relevant."

Prindabel's flurry of writing ground to a halt. Then he turned over his sheet of paper, printed something calmly on the other side and held it up. It said in big capital letters, 'We're stuffed'.

No one said anything as we each struggled to find a way to rebut the persuasiveness of Prindabel's last point.

"I reckon science fiction and fantasy films are relevant. You know a lot of them show what could happen in the future if we don't deal with the problems we have today. Bit like a warning. Like, have you ever seen *Gattaca*?... Well, it's about the dangers of cloning and genetic engineering – *Jurassic Park* does that too... and *Terminator* sort of shows the danger of relying too much on machines and computers... Oh, and Ignatius... you mentioned *Lord of the Rings*... Well, it's about standing up to evil and forgetting about differences and helping each other and about war, and that stuff's relevant today, isn't it?... and even *Spiderman*... couldn't you say it shows how scientific experiments can go wrong and how we have to be careful about...?"

Bill Kingsley stopped, not because he had run out of things to say, but because there were three faces gawking at him as if he had just stepped out of the mother ship.

"What? What's the matter?"

Razza leaned in for a closer look. "Who *are* you and what have you done to Bill Kingsley?"

It wasn't just the shock of hearing Bill speak or the fact that he was almost animated that had stunned us – it was more the realisation that what he was saying actually seemed to be making some sense.

"Bill, what about the other fantasy-type stuff like *Harry Potter*? Do you think that's relevant to... what was it... the problems facing today's world?" I asked, reading from the topic sheet.

"Well, I guess you could say that part of it's about how power can be used in a good way or a bad way and you could tie that to things like the power that big companies or politicians or dictators have today, I suppose. And Harry himself faces a lot of problems that I reckon would be relevant to a lot of people – you know, like coping with death and trying to fit in when you're different... and bullying. And Ignatius, you said films like that distract us from facing up to real problems, but maybe it's good to escape those problems – at least for a while – 'cause it might help people cope with them."

Bill Kingsley blinked and looked from Razza to Prindabel, who stared back at him as if he had just made an elephant appear in the room and they were trying to work out how he did it.

I wasn't staring, though. I was frantically trying to write down every word Bill Kingsley was saying. "Ignatius, Razza, don't just sit there. Ask Bill some more questions about the topic. Argue with him. Just keep him talking."

"Okay… what about all those superhero dudes with all their special powers?" Razza ventured. "What's that got to do with normal people and their problems?"

"But just about all of the superheroes are normal people most of the time and, like I said, it's how they use those powers that's the thing. And we have powers today that are pretty special and amazing, you know, with all the scientific discoveries going on, so maybe they're relevant because just like them, we have to choose how we're going to use our powers… I guess a bit like choosing between being superheroes or super villains."

"All right then," Prindabel joined in, "you said a lot of these films act as a warning to us today – give us some other examples?"

"There are loads. What about *I Robot* and the dangers of artificial intelligence or…"

"Yeah, that's right," Razza interrupted, still staring at Bill Kingsley in disbelief, "and what about that one where New York freezes over… you know, the *Morning After* or something…"

"*The Day After Tomorrow?*"

"Yeah, that's it… that's about global warming, isn't it? Cool!"

And that's the way it went for the next 20 minutes. Razza and Prindabel fired in questions and arguments, Bill Kingsley fired back answers and counter-arguments and I wrote it all down. When we didn't seem to be covering new ground I said, "I think we've got enough. There's a heap of rebuttal ideas, and I can divide Bill's main points up between the first and second speakers."

"Who *are* the first and second speakers?" Razza asked. "And who's taking Scobie's place?"

Prindabel shook his head. "Look, I'll go first speaker if you want me to, I will, but this isn't really my sort of topic. I mean it — I'd be better on the opposition's side. I really think Ishmael should be first speaker. He knows the team case — he's the one who's put it all together. Orazio, you should go second, and that leaves… Bill at third."

"Kingsley taking Scobie's place? No way, man. Have you forgotten that he can't rebut? And you want to put him in third speaker where that's exactly what he'll have to do — for just about his entire speech? No offence, Kingsley, but I don't think saying, 'That's quite a good point, actually,' is going to be enough to blow Preston's case out of the water. You're mad, Prindabel. Tell him, Ishmael."

"I think Ignatius is right."

Razza threw up his hands as if the world had turned insane.

"Look, we can't waste time on this," I said. "I should be first speaker because I know the overview of our case. Razza, you've been second speaker in three debates, so you should stick with that. That leaves third speaker. Ignatius has done his bit by helping us predict the opposition's arguments and giving us all the scientific stuff, but if it wasn't for Bill here we really would be stuffed. And you're wrong, Razza, he *can* rebut – maybe he hasn't ever done it before, but he's just spent the last 20 minutes rebutting everything you threw at him. He should be third speaker. This is his debate. And… I think he should be captain tonight, as well."

"Fine by me."

That was the easy part. Prindabel would agree with anything if it meant he didn't have to debate. All our eyes were now on Razza. He looked at me and then at Prindabel before turning patronisingly to Bill Kingsley.

"Billy Boy, you do appreciate the *seriousness* of the situation don't you – third speaker against Preston College… *Preston*? Remember what Prindabel said about drowning in our own offal? Well, that could be you. Do you understand how that would be a *bad* thing?"

Bill Kingsley glanced up at Razza. "Sure… even someone who had their brain removed by aliens and replaced with sludge could see that."

Razza frowned. "It could be very ugly out there."

Bill nodded. "It could be offal."

Had Bill Kingsley made a joke? Nah, we must have misheard.

"Don't you care?" Razza asked in exasperation. "This isn't some film, you know. We're not part of some whacky fellowship on some stupid quest. This is real. Aren't you just a teensy weensy bit... concerned?... worried?... nervous?... apprehensive?... scared out of your mind?"

"Of course," Bill said. "Look, I'll do whatever you want. If you just want me to be chair, that's fine. If you want me to go third speaker, that's fine too. I can't do what Scobie does... but I'll give it a go. Oh, and Orazio... I know we're not headed for Mount Doom or anything, but we *are* on a bit of a quest, aren't we? Maybe we're even some sort of a fellowship."

Razza sprawled back in his seat and shook his head slowly from side to side as if nothing made sense to him any more. Finally he stood up, leaned over the table and placed his hand on Bill's shoulder.

I held my breath. I had a terrible feeling that Orazio Zorzotto's razor-sharp wit was about to slice Bill Kingsley in two.

"A quest, you reckon?... And a fellowship?"

Bill shrugged and nodded slightly.

Razza fixed his eyes on the large form before him. "Then I will follow you," he said solemnly, "my brother... my *captain*... my... Kingsley."

36.
LIKE A LIGHT SABRE THROUGH BUTTER

At 7.25 p. m. we entered the debating room and took our seats. For the last half an hour we had frantically written up index cards and tried to get the key arguments in our minds. Now the horrible reality of what was about to happen hit home. The room was full. As well as an army of Preston supporters and the three adjudicators, St Daniel's was represented by my parents and Prue, along with Mr and Mrs Prindabel, Prindabel's sister, Mrs Zorzotto, Mr Kingsley, Miss Tarango, Brother Jerome and one of the school prefects.

I checked out the Preston team. Two girls and a boy sat opposite in dark coats and ties, staring at us like undertakers. It wasn't hard to work out whose funeral it was going to be.

Razza nudged my arm and passed a note. *It said, If you're thinking of going the grope again – the hot blonde is mine!* I gave him my best pained smile and looked down at Bill Kingsley. He was rocking back and forth and frowning. I didn't know if that was good or bad.

"Ladies and gentlemen…"

I jumped as Prindabel's voice cut across the room like a laser and the card Razza had just given me flicked from my hands, leaped into the air and sailed back over my head. I picked up my notes and drilled my eyes into them while my cheeks sizzled with embarrassment. The nightmare of the last debate came flooding back as I felt the whole room leaning in on me. I didn't really take in another word Prindabel said until he called on the first speaker for Preston, Razza's hot blonde, to start the debate.

It was obvious after about ten seconds that she was going to be way better than me. But the thing was, she wasn't perfect. She even looked a little nervous, and a couple of times she got a bit tangled up. I guess the short preparation ordeal was nerve-racking even for

Preston kids. I listened to her team outline and her main arguments and, thanks to Bill Kingsley, I knew I had a number of rebuttal points.

"... and that is why science fiction and fantasy films have little relevance to the problems facing today's world."

She sat down. A cement mixer had started up and was sloshing and churning away in my stomach. I waited as the adjudicators scribbled down notes and filled in their cards. Finally they exchanged glances and one of them nodded at Prindabel. This was it. The doors of the plane had burst open and I was looking down at the patchwork of land far below, wondering if I had remembered to pack my parachute.

"... first speaker for the Negative, Ishmael Leseur."

I stood up and walked to the front of the room. I forced myself to make eye contact with the audience. Mum stared, white-faced, as if I were about to perform open-heart surgery on myself with a blunt axe. Dad desperately tried to master the it's-no-big-deal-you'll-be-fine kind of expression but ended up looking as if he was having some kind of spasm. Prue suddenly seemed intensely interested in her fingers. Miss Tarango wrinkled her nose and nodded, and then turned the dimples on high beam.

I looked down at my first index card. This time I had written out the topic word for word so there would be no repeat of the last debacle. Then I noticed that something was scribbled below it. It said, *You da man, Ishmael! (Did you check your pants? Is Elvis in the undies?)*

I smiled, took a deep breath and began…

And would you believe it, when I'd finished, the entire audience stood and cheered and showered me with streamers and rose petals, and then the opposition team wept and conceded defeat and the adjudicators hoisted me on their shoulders and paraded me triumphantly around the room while I blew kisses, and on the front page of the paper the next day they wrote that I had made Martin Luther King's 'I have a dream' speech sound like a nursery recital and then the prime minister rang and begged me to be his PR man and the Pope…

No, I guess you wouldn't believe that, would you? You're right. To tell the truth, I was pretty ordinary. But I did manage somehow to mumble and stumble my way through, and I even succeeded in tearing my eyes away from my index cards and flashing them at the audience a few times. Not only that, I made it past the three-minute warning bell (though when it rang I got such a fright my voice cracked like a strangled chicken's and all the atoms in my body leaped apart for a nanosecond before clashing back together). Maybe I wasn't that brilliant, but on the positive side, I *had* remained conscious the entire time, I hadn't sexually assaulted a member of the opposition, and none of the world's most influential people had made a grand entrance via my shorts. Yeah, all in all, I was pretty happy.

I sat down with the last of the applause still clattering around me. Razza punched my shoulder and gave me some sort of weird handshake. Bill Kingsley patted me firmly on the back. I looked around the room. All the St Daniel's supporters were smiling and nodding at me like those little dogs in the back of cars. My parachute had finally exploded open and was yanking me into the clear blue sky.

It was only after the second speakers had completed their speeches that a startling thought began to take shape in my mind. We were actually doing all right. We weren't winning, of course, but we weren't getting thrashed, either. The way I saw it, the opposition were better speakers than us, but thanks to Bill, I thought we had a stronger case and better rebuttal. Amazingly, their second speaker didn't quite make the three-minute bell.

Even Razza seemed to sense something was happening and tried to put a lid on the jokes and smart comments. Only once did he stray, when he was making a point about how fantasies help people cope with real-life problems. "Everyone needs fantasy. We all fantasise some time. I know *I'll* be fantasising tonight," he said, leering at a certain Preston girl. I think 'mortified' is the word my mum would have used to describe her expression. But, apart from that little indiscretion, Razza stuck to the script and poured on the charm and flashed that winning smile as only the Big Z could.

The third speaker for Preston was confident, efficient and clinical. She was a definite future PM. Razza and I exchanged an oh-well-we-were-in-it-for-a-moment sort of look. Bill Kingsley was too busy to notice. He was listening intently. Every so often he would frown, shake his head vigorously as if he had taken some comment by the opposition as nothing less than a personal affront, and busily write on his index cards in incredibly small print. By the time the third speaker had finished, Bill had become so agitated that he stood up and went straight to the front of the room before she had even made it back to her seat. There he remained, tapping his index cards and staring impatiently at the adjudicators. Finally they gave the signal.

"To conclude the debate I would like to call…"

But Prindabel got no further. Bill Kingsley launched himself into his speech like a downhill skier. "How can the Affirmative team say that science fiction and fantasy films have little relevance to the problems facing today's world? Look at the arguments my team has presented…"

For the next 4 minutes Bill Kingsley argued and persuaded as if he had been waiting all his life just to make this speech. First he piled our main points one on top of the other until they seemed like a stone fortress, and then he cut through the opposition's case like a light sabre through butter. About 2 minutes in, he dumped his index cards on the chair's desk in frustration and continued without missing a beat. Soon the three-minute bell came and went and then the final four-minute bell rang twice. Just when it looked as if Bill Kingsley was as unstoppable as a runaway truck, Razza sneezed with all the force of an air-to-ground missile, "Aaaaaats-ennuuuufffff!"

Brother Jerome glared. The adjudicators raised their eyebrows.

Razza searched innocently for his handkerchief.

But it worked. Bill Kingsley stopped mid-sentence and looked around at the audience. "In conclusion… science fiction and fantasy are not just *relevant* to today's world, my team has shown tonight that they are *crucial*. In fact, it could be argued that once we stop imagining the future or *stop* fantasising about worlds different from the one we have today… that's when our real problems will *start*."

Bill Kingsley nodded earnestly, as if he was satisfied he had said his piece, and turned to go. Then the room erupted and the applause thundered on as he sat down. It was led by Razza, who was on his feet, whistling and whooping. I'm pretty sure this was a breach in debating etiquette, but the adjudicators were sharing a sly smile, so I hoped it would be overlooked.

There was nothing to do now but wait. A quiet

murmur slid around the room while the adjudicators tallied their marks and conferred. The Preston team looked a little rattled. They were whispering together, shaking their heads at times and shrugging their shoulders.

Razza nudged me in the ribs and jerked his head towards Bill Kingsley, who was gazing into space beside him. I knew what Razza was getting at. Bill looked different somehow. It must have been the smile on his face.

And the decision? Well, sorry, no Mighty Ducks' ending here. We lost the debate by one point. Two judges gave it to Preston by a point and one judge awarded a one-point victory to us. It was as close as that.

The thing was, though, none of us really cared. Honestly. We'd fronted up and given it our best shot. We hadn't drowned in our own offal. In fact, we had almost pulled off the impossible. We were happy with that. I think we all knew Preston were the better team and deserved to be in the final. We just got lucky with the topic.

I still think about that night all the time – I remember how everyone was smiling and congratulating us and saying how proud they were, just as if we had won.

Brother Jerome even called us 'true St Daniel's men'. And I remember how the Preston team came up and told us that they thought they had lost and we joked and talked together for a while and promised we would come and support them in the final. It was strange, but underneath all their coats and ties and braid and badges and stuff, they didn't seem that much different from us. And I remember, too, how Razza spent most of the time with his arm draped around Bill Kingsley's shoulder telling anyone who would listen, "I taught him everything he knows," until Brother Jerome said in his sternest voice, "Just as long as you didn't teach him how to sneeze, Mr Zorzotto." That broke everyone up.

But my favourite bit? My very favourite bit was when Miss Tarango came up to us and said, "You guys rock, you know that? You're my absolute heroes," and gave us each a hug. Razza winked at me and whispered, "She wants me," and laughed because even he didn't believe it. And then Miss Tarango stood right in front of Bill Kingsley and shook her head and said, "Billy, what can I say? Outstanding. You are my Jedi knight in shining armour," and Bill Kingsley seemed to swell up so much it looked as if he might explode.

I thought that night was going to be a disaster, but it ended up as one of the best nights of my life. The only way it could have been better was if Scobie could have been there to share it with us. I wondered about him later on as I lay in bed, too hyped up for sleep. What was he up to? Why hadn't he come back at the start of the term and what was he doing in Sydney with his father?

I just wished I knew what was going on.

The next day a letter arrived for me addressed in big, backward-sloping loopy writing. I guess sometimes you really should be careful what you wish for.

37.
PROBABLY
NOTHING

Inside the envelope I found a typed note.

Dear Ishmael,

There's been a bit of a problem and it looks like
I'm going to miss the debating finals.

It's that tumour operation we talked about. I have
these tests every six months to see if everything is still
all right – that it hasn't come back. They're no big
deal. It's just that this time, something showed up.
A 'shadow', they called it. They're not sure what it is
at this stage. They'll have to do more tests and scans,
but the doctors are confident that it's probably
nothing to worry about.

Don't know when I'll be back at school. Good luck in the finals. I'm counting on you to hold the team together.

James

PS Could you keep all this to yourself?

PPS Miss Tarango was right about words being powerful. Even words like 'probably' can hurt you.

After I read his letter I remembered what Scobie had said about the last operation using up all his fear. I wondered if that was true. I couldn't imagine what it would feel like being in his position and having to face it all again.

I guess it made Barry Bagsley seem like a minor skin irritation.

Part 4

... what trances of torments does that man
endure who is consumed with one unachieved
revengeful desire. He sleeps with clenched
hands; and wakes with his own bloody nails
in his palms.

HERMAN MELVILLE, *Moby Dick*

38.
WHO YA
GONNA CALL?

A few days after I received his letter, Miss Tarango announced to our Tutor Group that James Scobie wouldn't be returning to finish the year. She didn't go into any details. She just said it was for 'personal' and 'family' reasons.

Suddenly Barry Bagsley lurched back to life, as if he'd just had a million volts of electricity channelled through the bolts in his neck. "What are ya gonna do now, Le Turd, without that little freak to hide behind, hey? You got the guts to take me on all by yourself? Or are ya gonna go running to Barker and Jerome? Hey? Are ya? Or I know, maybe you and the other girls in your little debating club are planning on giving me a good talking to? Is that it? Hey? Hey?"

Barry Bagsley was certainly full of questions. Naturally, I countered his taunts with some pretty impressive eye avoidance and some stinging silence.

"Just as I thought. You're a gutless wonder without that little dork around, aren't you?"

Of course I could have pointed out that the 'little dork' he was referring to had kept him locked in his cage for half the year, but I decided this might be unwise. After a final parting shove, Barry Bagsley sauntered off as happy as a psychopath with a brand new chainsaw. The opportunities for mayhem must have seemed endless.

He took one of those opportunities the following week.

It was a Thursday, and it seemed to get off to a good start. At the assembly, all the members of the debating teams were presented with certificates of participation, and our team received a special one for making the finals. Brother Jerome gave a speech and said how impressed he was by our performance. We all left the hall feeling pretty good about ourselves. Bill Kingsley said it was the first certificate he had ever received. Prindabel said it was his forty-seventh. Razza told him that medical certificates didn't count.

Barry Bagsley struck that afternoon. Looking back, I guess all the warning signs were there during the lunch break. Danny Wallace and Doug Savage had been hanging around the lockers, and later both of them were huddled around Barry Bagsley at a computer in the library. That by itself should have been enough to set the alarm bells clanging. Barry Bagsley at a *computer*... in the *library*! My only excuse was that my radar had been dulled by my recent Barry Bagsley-free months.

It was after school that I came across Bill Kingsley at the lockers with his bag lying open at his feet and all his books and folders on the ground.

"What's up, Bill? Lost something?"

"Yeah, that debating certificate thing."

I must admit, this didn't particularly surprise me. Bill Kingsley was always losing stuff. Last year he spent an entire day looking for his 'good' pen until someone took pity on him and pointed out that it was behind his ear.

"Where'd you put it?"

"I'm sure I put it straight in my locker. I'm positive I did."

"Did you lock it?"

"I can't – lost my key last term."

"You can get a replacement, you know. Five bucks from Mr Grayson."

"I did. That's the one I lost."

"Oh… do you think someone might have nicked it?" I said, as the memory of Danny Wallace and Doug Savage skulking around this very spot flashed into my mind.

"Who'd want to steal a debating certificate – with my name on it?"

I had to admit he had a point there. "Have you checked your bag?"

"Yeah, it's not there."

"You sure you didn't take it to class?"

"I'm sure. I put it straight in my locker so I wouldn't lose it," he said dejectedly. "I wanted to show Mum and Dad."

"Maybe it got caught up in one of your books or one of your folders. We should check your desk just in case."

"All right," he agreed reluctantly, "but I bet it's not there."

He was wrong. That's exactly where it was. When Bill opened up his desk, the certificate leaped out at him. It had been pinned to the inside of the lid by two tacks. But its discovery didn't make Bill Kingsley happy. I watched as his face fell and his eyes clouded like molten glass. Someone had glued a picture of Jabba the Hutt right in the middle of his certificate and at the bottom some of the words had been crossed out and crudely written over. Now, instead of saying:

Awarded to: *William Kingsley*

For: *Reaching the Under Fifteen Debating Finals*

scrawls from a thick black pen had changed it to:

Awarded to: *William King-SIZE*

For: *being a fat turd!*

I looked at Bill. I remembered his face after that last debate. Now he looked numb and broken.

I ripped the certificate from the desk. "That's it. I'm taking this to Barker."

"No, Ishmael, don't!"

"Look, Bagsley and his lot did this. I know. I saw them hanging around the lockers today, then I saw them in the computer room – that's where they downloaded that picture. I'm not going to let them get away with it."

"Wait. Just forget about it, all right? It's only a bit of paper. It's not that important. It doesn't matter – just leave it."

"It *is* important. It *does* matter. Those idiots have got no right…"

"Look, Ishmael, it's *my* certificate, all right? It's not your problem. Just give it here… please."

I couldn't ignore the pain in Bill Kingsley's voice. I handed him the certificate. Without looking at it he screwed it up and stuffed it into his bag.

"They shouldn't get away with it, Bill."

"I don't care. No one else has to see it."

That afternoon we walked together in silence till we got to the bus stop.

"See ya tomorrow."

"Yeah, okay… and thanks for helping… you know, with the certificate and everything."

"Yeah… well…" There wasn't much else I could say. Some help I'd been. It seemed to me that every time I tried to help someone it ended badly. First I helped that primary school kid get his hat thrown in the creek, then I helped the debating team get beaten, *twice*, and now I'd helped Bill Kingsley to feel lousy about himself.

Something wrong in the neighbourhood? Who ya gonna call? Not me!

When I left Bill at the bus stop that day I vowed I would do two things. The first one was to ask Miss Tarango if she could make a replacement certificate. And the second thing? Well, my dad reckons that whatever you give out, you get back. "The bill always comes," he says. If you do good things, then good things come back. If you do lousy things, then they come back too. I don't know if that's true or not, but he believes it. He's told me plenty of times, "Don't ever think you've got away with anything or got something for nothing, because the bill always comes."

So that was the other thing I vowed I would do that day – make sure that Barry Bagsley paid for every lousy thing he'd done. It was just a matter of working out how I was going to deliver the bill.

39.
THE THIN
BROWN LINE

When I spoke to Miss Tarango about the new certificate she asked why Bill Kingsley hadn't seen her about it himself. I told her that he was too embarrassed because he was always losing stuff. That seemed to do the trick. She promised to have the replacement ready for me in a few days. As I was heading out to lunch I had another delightful encounter with Barry Bagsley.

"Hey, Le Turd, what's up your bum?"

I'm not sure, but I think that was an example of what Miss Tarango would call a mixed metaphor.

"Come on, Fish Dick, what's up? You don't look happy. You haven't had a fight with the other debating girls, have you? You can tell me. I'm *always* here to help," Barry Bagsley said, putting on a syrupy voice.

Apparently the anger that had been churning around inside me since the previous afternoon was pretty obvious. I spoke before I really knew what I was saying. "That was a shitty thing to do."

"Such language," Barry Bagsley said, covering his ears. "Whatever do you mean?"

"You know," I said, both angry and scared at the same time.

"No, why don't you tell me?"

I had started now and there was nothing I could do but go on. "What you did to Bill Kingsley – ruining his certificate."

"I don't know what you're talking about."

"Yes you do. I saw Wallace and Savage hanging around Bill's locker and I saw you all in the computer room."

"Just doing some extra study, that's all. I'd hate to think you were accusing us of some *foul play*, Le Turd. 'Cause if you are," he said, stepping in closer, "you better have some proof or you could get yourself in serious trouble."

"Why can't you just leave him alone?"

"Maybe I don't want to. Are you going to make me?"

And there it was. The question we'd all been waiting for. The question whose answer I knew, and Barry Bagsley knew, was "No". I looked at the smug, arrogant face before me, a face without a shadow of a doubt that it had nothing in the world to fear. I hated it and I hated how it was making me feel. I wanted to blow it away.

"What's he ever done to you?"

"Plenty. I have to look at all that blubber all the time and it puts me off my lunch. Besides, when he walks around I can't do my schoolwork because the whole building *shakes*, and he's always knocking my desk trying to squeeze all that lard down the aisle *and* his fat arse is always blocking out my view. So, Manure, I'll say and do whatever I want – unless, of course, you think you can stop me." He glared hard at me for a few seconds then gave a snort. "Just as I thought. You haven't got a prayer, Piss-whale. You have not got a prayer."

As Barry Bagsley walked away it was as if he had taken a part of me with him, torn a limb from my body and left me there bleeding.

I thought the feeling would go away the following

week after I slipped a brand new certificate into Bill Kingsley's bag during afternoon Tutor Group, but it didn't. And it still didn't go away the next day when Bill Kingsley thanked me and told me that his parents were having the certificate framed. I still felt as if a part of me was missing.

I tried to convince myself that everything was all right. After all, Bill Kingsley had his certificate back, so he was happy again, wasn't he? But the truth was, the look I saw on Bill's face that afternoon when he opened his desk hadn't really gone away. It was still there like a deep and ugly bruise. And there was something else, as well. After our little discussion, Barry Bagsley was directing more taunts Bill Kingsley's way, as if he was daring me to do something about it. Instead of helping Bill Kingsley, all I had done was make him a bigger target. It was as if I had thrown a lead weight to a drowning man.

I was still feeling bad the following week when Razza cornered me before school. "Ishmael, just the dude I wanted to see. You're going to come to the debating final Wednesday night, aren't you? Prindabel and Kingsley have jumped ship."

Going to a debating final was the last thing I felt like doing. "Look... I might give it a miss, too."

"What are you talking about? Come on, you gotta go."

"I don't know... I just..."

"What's the matter with you, anyway? You've been moping around like someone's superglued your bum shut."

First Barry Bagsley and now Razza. Why was it that whenever I looked a bit down everyone immediately assumed the problem originated from my backside? "It's nothing. Forget it."

"It's gotta be something. There are guys on death row chirpier than you."

"It's just..."

"Out with it, Leseur. You know that vee hef vays of may-kink you talk!"

There was no way Razza was going to be denied. I gave in and told him.

Razza took it all in without comment, then gave his considered opinion. "You're right. You're a menace to society. You should top yourself."

"Thanks, you've been a big help."

"Don't mention it," Razza said, before transforming into a voice-over man, "And after the break on Doctor Razz we'll continue our talk with young Ishmael Leseur, the boy who takes everything too seriously."

"Not everything's a joke, you know, Razza. Bill's not laughing."

"Look, you want to know the way I see it?"

"Have I got a choice?"

"Not really."

"Great, then. I'd *love* to know how you see it."

"Okay. Bagsley's a complete jerk, right?"

"Right." A no-brainer, that one.

"So who cares what a jerk says? You know what he calls me? Or-*arse*-i-*hole*. Or-arse-i-hole Zor-*zit*-to. Zit-arse for short. Has he cut me up? Am I wounded? Nuh, not a scratch. Now if my mum called me something like that… or you… that's different. But we're talking about Barry Bagsley here… and he's a loser, right?"

"Right." Maybe there was some truth in the old 'sticks and stones' argument for someone like Razza. You couldn't dent his confidence if you rammed it with a monster truck. I wondered if it was that easy for everyone.

"But it's not just the names. What he did to Bill Kingsley sucked."

"Yeah... yeah, you're right... so what do you wanna do? You wanna give him back some of his own medicine? You know, trash his stuff or something?"

A tempting thought, but realistically it didn't sound like a war we could win. "I don't think that's such a great idea."

"Well, there is another way," Razza said, quietly shifting his eyes from side to side. "We Zorzottos have *connections*, you know... back in Italy... *Sicily*... you get my drift? Just say the word, Ishmael, and your problem disappears, *poof!* Gone, forget about it. Or if that's a bit drastic, I'm sure we've got some old horses' heads lying around at home somewhere..."

"Thanks, Razz, but I might save that for my last resort," I said, hoping that he was joking.

"Well, if you won't listen to reason, I guess all I can say is, if you need me, I'll be there. I mean, if you have to take them on – Bagsley and that lot – I'll back you up, okay? Now, don't worry, I know what you're thinking, that the Razzman is a lover, not a fighter. But don't be fooled. When I was a little kid I was brought up on *Teenage Mutant Ninja Turtles*, so I know how to handle myself. I still have my Donatello costume at home if we need it. However, I should point out, that if it does come to serious fisticuffs, and my face is in danger of being marked in any way, I owe it to my legion of loyal female fans to get down on my knees and beg for mercy. Apart from that, I'll be right there with you, one hundred per cent. You and me, Ishmael, bricking ourselves – the thin brown line."

Razza just stood there, staring at me with that dopey know-it-all look on his face and bobbing his head up and down to some manic beat that only he could hear. At the debating semi-final Dad had called him "mad as a cut snake". Maybe he was, but I knew one thing about Orazio Zorzotto. If I really did need him, he *would* be there – one hundred per cent.

"What time does the final start?"

"Seven. Mum's dropping me off and I'm ringing her when it's finished. We can pick you up at your place at 6.30. You in?"

"Razza, this has nothing to do with debating, has it? It's all about that Preston girl, isn't it – the blonde one?"

"Yeah, of course," he said happily.

"Then why do you need me? I thought the Razzman was a bit of a superhero with the chicks."

"Yeah, well, that might be a *slight* exaggeration. Besides, even superheroes need their sidekicks, you know, to sort of make us look good in comparison. You'd be wicked at that. It could be your special calling."

"Gee, thanks."

"Don't mention it. So? Are you coming or what?"

Sidekick for the Razzman. There were worse jobs.

"I'll be there," I said, "one hundred per cent."

40.
LIKE ICE CREAM
IN A MICROWAVE

In the end I was kind of glad I went to the debating final. Of course I had to battle to contain Razza, who tended to be a tad over-vigorous in his support, particularly when a certain blonde-haired speaker was on. But all in all it was a pretty exciting night, and ended with Preston defeating Colmslie College in front of a big crowd.

Afterwards Razza dragged me up and we congratulated the Preston team on their victory. I tried to be a good sidekick by keeping quiet and letting Razza have the floor (not too difficult for me) and laughing at all his jokes. It seemed to work fairly well. After a while, when the rest of the team began to break away and mingle with the crowd, Razza still had his 'hot blonde' cornered. I took that as my cue to leave and headed out to a big courtyard area and the refreshments. The other years' finals had also just finished, and people were still spilling from nearby rooms. I grabbed an orange juice and found myself a quiet spot to wait for Razza.

I wasn't alone for long.

"Ishmael?"

I turned in the direction of the voice.

"Hi, look, you probably don't remember me, but I'm Kelly Faulkner."

It was Kelly Faulkner. I stared at her. Kelly Faulkner was talking to me. There was Kelly Faulkner and there was me. We were both standing there. Me and Kelly Faulkner. I stared at her. Kelly Faulkner was talking to *me*. It was *Kelly Faulkner*! Why was she looking at me like that?

"We debated against each other?" She frowned a little and gave a weak smile.

Oh god, she thought I didn't remember her. And no wonder, I'd been staring at her like a moron. I tried to speak, but someone had put my brain in the blender and selected 'puree'. "No... yeah... yes... no... we... I... I did... I do... we did... that's right... you... yeah... that's right... debate... yeah..." No, I wasn't quoting Shakespeare. This was all my own work. What I desperately needed was my own sidekick to help make *me* look good – a trained baboon, perhaps? No, not trained – too much competition.

"I was going to catch you after the debate but... well... I didn't get a chance."

The horrible memories of that night came flooding back like sewage into a septic tank.

"No... I... it... I..." How could I put this? "I... was pretty bad." Have I introduced myself? I'm Ishmael Leseur, master of the understatement. You remember me, I'm the guy who said Jack the Ripper lacked people skills.

"Don't say that... it could have happened to anyone."

"You really think so?" I asked hopefully.

"Well..." she said with a crooked grin, "maybe not that bit with the peg."

"No... it... I..." But that was as far as I got. What possible explanation could make a clothes peg falling from your pants during a debate seem fine and dandy?

"It looked like... it had a... *face*... drawn on it?"

Kelly Faulkner asked delicately, as if she was enquiring as to whether or not I suffered from piles.

I nodded. Perhaps a little trivia would help my case. "It was Ringo... from the Beatles." Yes, well, that explained everything. Of course! Who wouldn't have had a peg figure of the drummer from a 1960's band shoved up their shorts during a debate? It stands to reason.

"Oh... right," she said, with the look of someone who had just found herself alone in a lift with an axe murderer.

"It got... caught up, somehow," I tried to explain, "... from our clothes line. It's full of the world's most influential people."

"Really?" Make that an axe murderer with bad breath and BO.

"They're my sister's. She makes them."

"Does she?"

"Yes – she's almost a genius."

"Really?"

That's right, and her brother's a complete cretin, otherwise he would shut his mouth and realise that he had been making a much better impression when he was just staring at Kelly Faulkner like a moron.

I stared at Kelly Faulkner like a moron.

"Well, anyway," she said, stung into action by the power of my moronic stare, "I think you did well, you know, stepping in at the last moment. I don't think I could do that. I'd be hopeless."

"You couldn't have been worse than me," I said. "I bet you wouldn't have faint..." Suddenly I had a vision of Razza's face leering in at me and saying, *It looked like you were very keen to keep a-breast of the opposition's argument.* Oh my god! How could I have forgotten about that? That's probably why she was there – she was waiting for an apology, or maybe she'd come to inform me her father had a contract out on my life.

"Look, about the debate... when I... fainted... passed out... they said... they told me... I didn't know..."

Kelly Faulkner frowned and tilted her head on the side as she tried to make sense of the babbling crazy person in front of her.

"... my hand... when I fell..."

Suddenly her beautiful ice-blue eyes widened and her cute mouth formed into a perfect 'O'. "Oh... oh no... no, don't... it's..."

"I just wanted you to know that I didn't... I wasn't... I..."

"Don't... no... you don't..."

"I just... when I... my hand just..."

"No... no... really... don't... really..."

"I'm sorry... there's no way... I wouldn't... I couldn't... I didn't..."

"No, I know... I know... forget it... don't... it's not..."

"I just wanted you to know..."

"No... I know, I know..."

"I..."

"I *know*," Kelly Faulkner said firmly. Now she was staring at the ground and biting the side of her bottom lip. Her cheeks were dark pink blotches.

Something was trying to lever my ribs apart and escape from my chest.

She shook her head slightly. "Anyway, look... I really just came... to thank you."

Thank me? What was she thanking me for, passing out?

"You would have won anyway."

"What?" she said, lifting her head.

"You would have beaten us anyway, even if we didn't have to forfeit because of me."

"No... oh no... no. I wasn't talking about that. I wanted to thank you... for helping my brother."

"Your brother? But..."

"My little brother Marty. Some boys were teasing him down by the creek one day. I think you helped him. It *was* you, wasn't it?"

I felt like my head was stuck in the spin dryer. "That was your brother?"

"Yes, and what you did was great."

"But I... I really only helped him get his hat thrown in the creek."

"I think you did a little bit more than that. Marty told me all about it. He knew you went to St Daniel's but he couldn't remember your proper name – thought it was something about *mail*. He told me the other boys kept calling you all sorts of things like *Fish-whale*... and something about a *sewer*?"

I guess the look on my face told her it was true.

"Boys can be so charming," Kelly Faulkner said knowingly.

I wanted to tell her that some of us could be,

we really could, if only we were given the chance.

"Anyway, that night when I saw your name on the board, I thought it had to be you. I wanted to ask you about it after the debate, but... well... like I said, I didn't get a chance. When I got home I told Marty, and he remembered the *Ishmael* part. I didn't think there'd be too many Ishmaels around the place."

"No, it's a pretty stupid name, all right."

"Stupid? I don't think so. I wish I had a more interesting name. Kelly Faulkner's pretty plain."

"No way... no it's not. It's perfect... it suits you."

"Don't know about that," she said, shaking her head shyly.

"Well, I'd give anything for an ordinary name. Something like John or Dave, *anything* but Ishmael. I hate it."

"Hate it? Why?"

I didn't think that Kelly Faulkner was quite ready to hear all my theories about Ishmael Leseur's Syndrome. "I don't know, I just hate it. I wish my dad had never read *Moby Dick*."

"*Moby Dick*? What's that got to do with it?"

"That's where he got *Ishmael* from. It's the name of

one of the main characters in the book – the narrator."

"What's he like?"

"My father?"

"No – *Ishmael* – the person you're named after."

"Oh yeah, right," I said, feeling like a dork.

"Well?"

"What… oh… I don't know what he's like. I've never read it."

"Really? You haven't read it? How come? If I was named after someone in a book I'd definitely want to read it to find out what they were like. You know, see if I was like them. I can't *believe* you haven't read it."

Did I say I felt like a dork? Make that a double-dork.

"I've read the first line." Oh, well done, Einstein. How's that Theory of Relativity going? Got the first letter worked out yet?

"The first line?" she said, curling up her top lip and cranking my heartbeat up another notch.

"That's where the name comes in," I explained, desperately trying to perform CPR on what remained of my rapidly fading dignity. "*Call me Ishmael*. That's how it starts. It's the first line. Apparently it's pretty famous. And that's another thing I hate about my name.

Call me Ishmael. For the rest of my life, I know that there will always be some clown who's read *Moby Dick*, and when they hear my name, they just won't be able to resist blurting out *Call me Ishmael!* like they're the first person in the entire universe to think of it, and they'll think they're just so brilliant and hilarious."

"It can't be that bad," Kelly Faulkner said sympathetically.

"It is. Seriously, the next time someone comes out with that *Call me Ishmael* line, I'll scream. I will. I mean it. The very next time I get a *Call me Ishmael* I'm just going to scream. I'm not kidding."

"I believe you," Kelly Faulkner said, holding up her hands and pulling one of those beautiful, funny faces that just kill me. "Look, I've got to go. I have to find my little sister. Her team got through to the finals too for her age group – they lost, unfortunately. I'm glad I got the chance to thank you. I think it was really brave of you to stand up to those three boys like that and…" She stopped mid-sentence and looked past my shoulder. "Do you know that guy?"

I turned around. It was Razza. He was jumping about and shooting his fingers at me like he was one of the

Wiggles. His mouth was forming the words *You da man* over and over again.

"No," I said, turning back. "Never seen him before in my life."

Kelly Faulkner stared at Razza and wrinkled her nose. "But wasn't he in your debating team?"

I followed the line of her eyes. "Oh *him*," I said pathetically. "Yes, I know *him*."

"Is he a friend of yours?" Kelly Faulkner said, blinking her eyes in disbelief as Razz attempted his own version of the moonwalk and ended up colliding with a not-very-impressed woman carrying a tray of drinks.

"Unfortunately, yes."

"What *exactly* is he doing?"

At that particular moment Razza was staggering about and grasping his chest as if Cupid had just skewered him with a high-jump pole.

"It's difficult to explain."

"I imagine it would be."

"Unfortunately he suffers from a rare brain condition."

"Really?"

"Yes, he doesn't have one."

And then it happened. Kelly Faulkner laughed

and her beautiful pale blue eyes melted my heart like ice cream in a microwave till all that remained was an awful empty feeling. That's when I knew. Nothing would ever happen between us. I'd been kidding myself. It just wasn't possible for eyes as beautiful as that to see anyone as ordinary as me. For the first time I didn't feel like a nervous wreck in Kelly Faulkner's presence. What did I have to worry about? "When you ain't got nothin' you got nothin' to lose," Bob Dylan had wailed hundreds of times from my father's CD. Well, no one had more nothin' than me. I looked at Kelly Faulkner and said the first thing that came into my head.

"Do you want to know a secret? That guy's really a superhero."

"Is that right?" Kelly Faulkner said, raising her eyebrows and looking impressed.

"Yes, but the thing is, in order to keep his identity hidden, he has to pretend that he's a complete idiot."

"He's doing a wonderful job."

"Nobody does it better."

She pushed up her bottom lip and nodded thoughtfully. "I've never seen a real live superhero before. How come you know his identity?"

"Well, I shouldn't really be telling you any of this…
but I'm his sidekick."

"Wow, pretty impressive. So you guys go round
solving crime, rescuing babies from burning buildings,
saving damsels in distress, everyday chores like that?"

"We do what we can."

"And I suppose that you have cool costumes like
Spiderman or the Phantom?"

"Not really – neither of us can sew."

"That's a shame. Any super powers, then? You know,
to help you combat all those evil villains?"

"Well, I don't have any personally, but he has the
power to talk people to death… and I know from
personal experience that his jokes can make you want
to throw yourself under a train."

"Impressive. And does he have a name – like a proper
superhero name, I mean?"

"Sure. He's the Razzman."

"The Razzman, eh? Not bad. And what about you?
What's your name?"

"Sidekicks don't get to have cool names."

"That doesn't seem fair."

"Comes with the territory."

Kelly Faulkner gave me a knowing smile. As I looked at her I thought that there ought to be a law against anyone being that beautiful, especially around people like me. Perhaps it comes under cruelty to dumb animals.

"Well, I really better go and let you guys get on with saving the world. Thanks again for helping Marty out. Hey, you know, after what you did, maybe you should apply for a promotion from sidekick? I could write you a reference." She held her hand up near her face and wiggled her fingers. "See ya."

She didn't have time to leave, however, before Razza came bounding in and leaped on me like I had just scored the winning goal in the FA Cup Final. "How you doing?" he said to Kelly Faulkner at the same time as he was half-strangling me. "I'm the Razzman."

"I know," she whispered, glancing around furtively, "but don't worry... your secret's safe with me." Then she zipped her lips, locked them with an imaginary key and disappeared into the crowd.

I stared at the big empty space where, moments before, Kelly Faulkner had been standing. It matched the one inside my chest.

41.
THE KING OF DROOL

"**Y**ou rescued her little brother from Bagsley and his mob?"

Razza and I were waiting for Mrs Zorzotto and he was gawking at me like I had two heads.

"I think 'rescued' might be pushing it a bit."

"Mate, doesn't matter what *you* think. It's what *she* thinks, and I'm telling you, you're in. You *saved* her little brother," he repeated, almost in disbelief. "You're a knight in shining armour. That's *gold*, mate – chick-winning gold! You are in, you are definitely *in*!"

"Look, I didn't have a clue it was her brother,

and anyway – they chucked our hats into the creek. Some rescue… some hero."

"Don't you get it? That's even better – that makes you a nice guy who goes around helping complete strangers, sacrificing himself for others. Chicks *love* that corny stuff." Razza beamed at me like I'd just won the Lottery. "Man, I'm telling you, you are so in! No wonder she was drooling all over you."

"Drooling? You're mad."

"It's true. You can't fool the Razz. I'm the King of Drool. It's what I do… and I recognise drool in others."

"Okay, you can stop right there. I think I'm going to be sick."

"I'm just saying that on the outside she looked all *cool*, but on the inside she was all *drool*."

Another disturbing image flashed in my mind. It was time to put a stop to this before it got out of control. "Look, Razza, she just wanted to thank me, that's all. She's probably forgotten all about me already, so let's drop it, eh? And there was no *drooling*, all right? Kelly Faulkner doesn't *drool*. She was just being nice. She can't help but be nice. She is nice. She was born with an excess of the niceness gene. She probably just felt sorry for me. That's all. I'm *nothing* to her and nothing's going to happen. And you know why? Because she's perfect *and* she's got a *personality*, for god's sake. Compared to her, I'm a lump of wood. So I've got no chance with her, okay? Do you understand? No chance. Zero! Zilch! Can I make it any clearer to you than that?"

Razza stared at me seriously and slowly nodded, "Yeah... I reckon you're *definitely* in."

My only hope was to change the subject, preferably to one that really interested him. "Anyway, what about you? You never told me what happened with you and that blonde girl."

"Oh her. It's over," Razza said casually.

"Over?!"

"Yeah, it was good while it lasted, but you know, I think it was time to pull the pin."

"Good while it lasted? You've only spoken to her twice. What happened?"

"Well, there was a bit of a problem."

"What kind of a problem?"

"Irreconcilable differences."

"What?"

"Irreconcilable differences… you know, things that just can't get worked out… like with Mum and the old man," Razza said, shuffling his feet and kicking at a stone.

"But what irreconcilable differences could you have after only speaking to her for 15 minutes?"

"Well, it *appears*," said Razza thoughtfully, as if he were a doctor diagnosing a rare condition, "that I like *me*… and she *doesn't*."

"Oh… right. I can see how that could lead to problems in the relationship. Sorry."

"No problem. Probably for the best," Razza said philosophically. "I was starting to feel trapped – you know, tied down? Our… *relationship*… was becoming… well, *predictable*. I need my freedom. You hear what I'm saying?"

I nodded and Razza continued grandly.

"Sure, we had our good times – the laughter, the tears – but I think we both realised it was time to move on. Besides, it's not right to selfishly restrict myself to one chick and deny all those other gorgeous babes the pleasure of my company."

"You're a real humanitarian, do you know that?"

"No, please, don't embarrass me. I'm just one little person trying to make a difference."

"You're way too modest."

"Yes, I know," Razza said, sighing and shaking his head regretfully, "but it's my *only* failing."

Just then Mrs Zorzotto pulled up across the road.

"Look, Ishmael, I still think you should go after that Kelly chick," Razza said as we headed towards the car. "Why don't you find out her number and give her a bell? What have you got to lose?"

"Nah, forget it."

"I could help you, you know – give you the benefit of my vast experience."

"Geez, that's a tempting offer," I said. "Imagine, the King of Drool in *my* corner. What an honour. Kelly Faulkner would be like putty in my hands."

"Exactly!" Razza shot back enthusiastically as we jumped into the back seat of his mother's car.

At home that night I made up my mind about a couple of things. Firstly, I decided, despite what Razza might think, it was time to put Kelly Faulkner back where she belonged, back where impossible things could happen – in my fantasies and daydreams. She really wasn't the kind of person who could exist in the real world... not in my real world, anyway. The second thing I decided to do was ask Dad if I could borrow his copy of *Moby Dick*.

"Aaarrrgh, me hearty," he said, rolling his eyes crazily, "ye be seeking the white whale!"

I wasn't, though. I be seeking Ishmael.

42.
THE REAL DEAL

Reading *Moby Dick* wasn't quite as straightforward as I thought it would be. For a start, when I asked Dad about borrowing a copy, he insisted that I had to read the 'real deal', not the 'kiddies' version', as he put it.

The real deal turned out to be a thousand pages of small print – six hundred pages of story, *plus* another *four hundred* pages of notes and commentary that, thankfully, my father said I could afford to skip. I'm here to tell you, if you want to know *anything*, and I mean anything, about whales and whaling, then check out *Moby Dick*. It is the whale heads' bible.

I started it that night after I got home from the

debating finals. I held the book like a chunky brick in my hands. Somehow it made me feel like there was a connection between Kelly Faulkner and me. I turned to the first page. *Call me Ishmael*, it said, and I waded in like I was heading out to sea.

I have to confess that at times it was a pretty hard slog. I reckon Miss Tarango would have a thing or two to say to old Herman about editing – there's only so much a person needs to know about the history and techniques of whaling or the workings of whaling boats or the bone structure and internal organs of whales themselves. Still, if I'm ever on *Who Wants to Be a Millionaire* and Chris asks a question about the average weight of blubber found in a fully grown sperm whale, I'll be laughing, right?

Despite all that, I still got caught up with the story, and just like Ishmael, his strange friend Queequeg and the rest of the crew of the *Pequod*, I found myself drawn into Captain Ahab's mad quest for revenge against the white whale, which had reduced his personal leg stockpile by fifty per cent. By the time I was halfway through, one thing was obvious to me: I was nothing like this Ishmael. Sure, we both had pretty weird friends, but apart from that, as Dad would say, we were as different as 'chalk and cheeseburger'.

Now don't get me wrong. It's not like I expected us to be identical twins or anything. It did dawn on me that being a fourteen-year-old boy still at school and living in the twenty-first century might tend to make me *slightly* different from a grown man on a whaling boat in the 1800s. I just thought that maybe there would be some similarities between us. But was there a Barry Bagsley clone on board *Pequod* whose life's ambition was to make Melville's Ishmael feel like a loser with about as much backbone as a jellyfish? Uh-uh. Did the other Ishmael ever suffer anything remotely embarrassing like fainting when he came face to face with his first whale? Absolutely not. Did he ever have to deal with something totally humiliating like, say, a stray harpoon dropping from his whaling britches just as he was about to perform a sea shanty for the crew? Not a chance. Did he ever find himself slipping on whale oil or tripping over loose rigging, and in trying to break his fall, discovering to his surprise that he had accidentally groped Captain Ahab in a way that could lead to charges of sexual harassment or, worse still, an audience with the plank? No way José!

You see, the plain truth was, unlike me, the Ishmael

in *Moby Dick* wasn't a loser at all. He certainly wasn't cursed by Ishmael Leseur's Syndrome. He didn't even *have* a last name – I guess that's what saved him. No, the further I read into the book, the more I was convinced we had nothing in common whatsoever. But there was someone else on board the *Pequod* who I *could* relate to. Maybe I hadn't lost my leg to a great white whale like he had, but I understood what it was like to have a part of yourself torn away and I also knew how much you could grow to hate whoever or whatever it was that had taken that part from you. I knew all about that, because every time Barry Bagsley taunted me and ground my name into the dirt, and every time he had a go at Bill Kingsley and I did nothing, it felt like there was much more of me missing than just a limb. But was I really like Ahab? Did I crave revenge like him? Would I really like to hunt down Barry Bagsley and harpoon him and make him suffer for what he had done?

You bet.

And that feeling continued to spread inside me like a virus. Not that I'm blaming Herman Melville at all. It wasn't reading about Captain Ahab that made me feel that way. It was because back at school, Barry Bagsley was increasing his attacks on Bill Kingsley. It seemed that every time Bill opened his desk or locker he would be confronted by some cruel image – a sumo wrestler, a blimp or the 'before' shot from a weight-loss ad – along with some scribbled insult. As fast as he tore them down and slung them in the bin, new, more outlandish ones would replace them. And it wasn't just the pictures and drawings. Bagsley and his friends now made pig-grunting noises whenever they passed within earshot.

What really stoked the fire for revenge that raged in my belly was that after every taunt, Barry Bagsley would smirk in my direction as if he was daring me to do something about it. I wanted to do something, I really did. I tried to convince Bill to let Mr Barker know what was going on, but there was no way he would be in on it. "Great, then I'd get to be a dobber as well," he replied miserably. "Look, Bagsley will get sick of it after a while. Forget it – I'm fine."

He didn't look fine though, and Barry Bagsley's campaign showed no signs of relenting. As we crawled towards the end of the school year, Bill Kingsley began to wear the desperate look of a wounded beast hounded by a pack of wild dogs.

43.
WIRED AND
TICKING

It was the second to last week of the year, and things weren't exactly going swimmingly. Besides the continuing disappointment of Barry Bagsley's name failing to turn up on the Ten Most Wanted List, I also found myself buried under an avalanche of exams and assignments. Then, just to add to my joy, Mr Barker informed the members of the Under Fifteen debating team that we would all be 'volunteering' to be readers at the traditional end-of-year assembly/mass/prize-giving/ speech night/ extravaganza thingy. Wonderful. Now I could be embarrassed and humiliated on a grand scale.

The end-of-year assembly/mass/prize-giving/speech night/extravaganza thingy was always held on the

Thursday night of the last week of school – with Friday being the first day of the Christmas holidays. Naturally everyone was expected to attend, and in a remarkable display of school spirit, nearly everyone always did. (Of course, the fact that those who failed to attend had to come to school the next day or face two weeks of afternoon detentions the following year might have had something to do with it as well.)

As Mr Barker informed us, our job on the night was to read out the Prayers of Petition – you know, where you ask for all those really important things that will probably never happen, like world peace, the elimination of poverty and hunger from around the globe, freedom for all people and a premiership for the St Daniel's First Fifteen. For days, the awful thought of speaking in front of well over a thousand students, teachers and parents kept exploding into my mind like an airbag in a Mini. That was, until the day Bill Kingsley presented his Citizenship oral. After that there wasn't much room left in my mind for anything else but revenge.

The Citizenship orals had been going all week, and Mr Barker's limited patience and good humour seemed to be shrivelling up with each presentation. Our task was to *Examine the Liveability of Your Suburb*, and I had to admit that the standard wasn't exactly world-class.

Razza reckoned Prindabel's talk was so boring it could have put coffee to sleep. Razza's own talk, however, seemed based on the assumption that the liveability of a suburb was in direct proportion to the number of 'hot chick schools' that were within a 1-kilometre radius.

Danny Wallace's talk was so short, Mr Barker said that his suburb "would appear to have the liveability of a morgue". The highlight of Doug Savage's presentation was his conclusion that his suburb was extremely liveable because "everyone living there was alive", while Barry Bagsley expressed the bewildering opinion that "no one would be seen dead living in my hole of a suburb".

By the time it was Bill Kingsley's turn to speak, Mr Barker was well and truly wired and ticking.

It's not that Bill Kingsley hadn't done any work. In fact, he had probably done more work than anyone else in the class. He had been determined to show that his success in the debating finals wasn't a fluke. I knew for a fact that every day of the previous two weeks he had spent lunchtimes and after school working in the library doing research and putting together a PowerPoint presentation. A couple of times Bill had even practised his talk on me. Now I'm no teacher, but I reckon it was definitely 'A' material.

Bill started off well. He introduced his report and clicked up the first slide showing *Criteria for Assessing Liveability*.

"First I will examine in detail the recreation and entertainment facilities that contribute to the liveability of my suburb of Carrington."

Then things went pear-shaped. When Bill clicked to the next slide, a photo leaped on to the screen of an enormous woman whose body was swallowing her bikini. Underneath was the caption, *When the whale-watching season begins this summer, make sure they're not watching you. Join Flab-Busters now!*

Those in the class who hadn't yet gone into a coma sputtered with laughter.

"Quiet!" Mr Barker growled.

Bill quickly clicked to the next slide and a list of bus and train services appeared.

"Kingsley, what exactly are you doing? Is this some kind of joke?"

"No, no sir... I, I must have got the slides mixed up or something..."

"Well, son, just get on with it, will you? Put us all out of our misery."

I looked to the back corner of the room. Barry Bagsley's face was split in a smug grin while Danny Wallace and Doug Savage were sprawled on the desk behind him, stifling their laughter.

Bill tried to continue his speech but now his slides were out of sequence and you could tell that his confidence was shaken. He pointed the remote control at the laptop in front of him. *Click.* An ad for Weight Watchers. *Click* again. An upside-down graph titled *Population Growth for Carrington.* Bill was flustered. He shuffled through his index cards, and in the process spilled half on the floor. As he disappeared behind a desk to retrieve them, a mixture of groans and laughter poured down on him.

Mr Barker held his head in his hands.

Bill struggled to his feet and grabbed the remote again. *Click.* An ad for Jenny Craig. *Click.* A picture of the backside of a hippopotamus. *Click.* A giant bloated pig. *Click.* I'm not sure but... *Click.* Was that a...? *Click.*

Click. Click. Click. Click. And *Click. Criteria for Assessing Liveability.*

"Mr Kingsley, were you on some kind of hallucinogenic drug when you put this presentation together?"

"No, sir."

"Well, son, you've had weeks to get this sorted out, but you've obviously wasted your time daydreaming as usual. Now if you want any sort of grade at all, I suggest you start immediately or I will have to fail you for being unprepared. Do I make myself clear?"

Bill turned off the computer and continued his talk, but his voice was just a droning mumble and he made no effort to sort out his index cards as he drifted from one unrelated point to another. Finally, when he was less than halfway through, he flipped through the remaining cards and shook his head hopelessly. "That's about it, I guess," he said, and sat down.

Mr Barker squeezed the skin on his forehead, scribbled a letter on the bottom of Bill Kingsley's mark sheet and circled it with a flourish. Even from the other side of the room I could tell it was a 'D'.

After the lesson, as everyone escaped to lunch, I stayed at my desk.

"Hey, Ishmael. Whatta you doing? Having a party with all your friends?" It was Razza. "Earth to Ishmael. Can you read me?"

"Bill *was* prepared. He had that speech perfect – Bagsley stuffed it up."

"Then Kingsley should tell someone – tell Barker."

"You know he wouldn't do that."

"Then we'll tell him."

"What good would that do? Bagsley would get in trouble, get some more detentions and then they'd find other ways to make Bill's life hell. And the teachers won't have a clue what's going on."

"Then what do you want to do?"

"I want to get him – I want to make him pay big time," I said through clenched teeth.

"Sure, but how? I mean, you're not thinking of doing anything stupid, are you?"

"What? Like putting a contract out on him? Slipping a horse's head into his bed?"

"Yeah, well, I was just joking about that stuff. You know me, right, always kidding. Look, Ishmael, I think you're letting this get to you too much. Why don't you just forget about all this crap? Bagsley's just not worth it."

"No, you're right, he's not... but Bill is. There's gotta be something we can do to help him."

Razza looked at me and for the first time I could remember his face seemed serious. "Leave it with me."

"But what can you do?"

"Haven't got a clue – yet. But you know what they say, the Razzman works in mysterious ways."

Actually, I had no idea that they said that (or for that matter, who 'they' were) and I was about to point this out when Barry Bagsley bounded through the door, wrenched open the lid of his desk and scooped up a football. It wasn't until he turned to leave that he even noticed there was someone else in the room.

"Well, well, if it isn't Le Spewer and Zit-arse. What are you girls up to?"

Neither of us replied.

"What's the matter, Or-*arse*-i-*hole*? You've always got plenty to say. You look a bit upset. Don't tell me you wet your bed again last night?"

"No way!" Razza said, looking genuinely horrified. "I haven't done that for weeks. I'm cured. I have total control of my bladder. Now I only wet the bed when *I* want to," he said proudly.

Barry Bagsley stared at Razza like he was from outer space. "You're an idiot, Zorzotto, you know that."

Razza smiled. "You think so?" he replied pleasantly, while holding Barry Bagsley's stare. "It's hard for me to know. I've heard that the individual is not the most reliable judge of their own sanity."

They remained locked together for a few seconds, then Barry Bagsley shifted his eyes to me. "And what's your problem, Manure? You're not crying about Billy Kingsize and his piss-weak presentation, are you? It's his own fault. You heard Barker, he just wasn't prepared. Shocking."

"He *was* prepared," I spat back, "but *someone* got at his work."

"Really? Well, I'll tell you what you should do, Manure. You should find that *someone* and have a word with them."

"I *am*."

Suddenly it felt like some line had been crossed, some step taken that couldn't be taken back.

"Is that right?" Barry Bagsley said, moving closer and tossing the football from hand to hand. "And what exactly are you saying then?"

"Leave Bill Kingsley alone."

"Well that's a beautiful thought, Manure, but the tricky question is, how are you going to make me?"

Barry Bagsley stood a metre from me, his face hard and cold like concrete. Then his hands shot forward as if he was going to throw the football into my face. "Boo!" he shouted at the same time. I grimaced and jerked my hands up. He laughed and spun the football on one finger. "You haven't got a prayer, Manure," he said cheerfully before underlining his claim by poking my chest in time to each word. "Have – not – got – a – prayer."

I watched as he strutted from the room. My hands were cramped into tight fists. My fingernails stabbed into my palms.

"I doubt if he'll mess with us again," Razza said knowingly.

44.
EVERY LOST
BATTLE

That weekend I read the final chapters of *Moby Dick*. When I gave the copy back to Dad, he insisted that I had to see the video of the movie – the old one starring Gregory Peck as Ahab.

On Sunday afternoon, I watched the final dramatic battle unfold on the screen. I saw a fearsome Moby Dick destroy the *Pequod* and send her crew to their deaths. I saw Captain Ahab trapped in a tangle of harpoon ropes, lashed to the side of the great white whale, striking out in anger and hatred to the very end, even as the massive beast dragged him to a watery grave. And finally, when all seemed lost, I saw Ishmael bobbing on the surface of the ocean gasping for air – the sole survivor of Ahab's quest for revenge. I was right – he was nothing like me.

I had a strange dream that night. It started off at school. At first I was in a normal class, but somehow it turned into some sort of a swimming pool, only I still had my school uniform on. Then I heard someone calling out my name. I turned around and there was Barry Bagsley. He had Bill Kingsley by the hair and he was pushing him under the water. He smiled at me and held Bill under. I yelled at him to let go but he just laughed. I tried to hit him, but he ducked out of the way and laughed even more. All the time Bill's arms were thrashing and air bubbles were boiling to the surface.

Then Barry Bagsley puffed up his cheeks and began to sink down into the water, taking Bill Kingsley with him. I screamed at him to stop, but he kept the same stupid grin on his face as he disappeared below the surface. I was desperate now. I leaped on Barry Bagsley and wrapped my arm around his throat. I didn't know if I was trying to pull him to the surface or strangle him. But it didn't make any difference. I gulped in some air before I was dragged underwater.

As we sank deeper and deeper, I squeezed Barry

Bagsley's throat with all my might and struck his face, but it didn't bother him at all. He just laughed and repeated over and over, "You haven't got a prayer. You haven't got a prayer," as bubbles streamed from his mouth. Then it became really weird. Barry Bagsley turned into some kind of mutant fish and slipped from my grasp, so I grabbed Bill Kingsley by the arm, but he started to blow up like a balloon, only he got heavier instead of lighter. He was dragging us both down. Everything became colder and darker and my lungs burned like they were on fire. The last bubbles of air were escaping from my mouth.

Then I woke up.

I didn't sit bolt upright in bed like people do in the films when they have nightmares, but I did shudder a little from the effort of making myself wake up, and my heart and lungs seemed to be fighting each other to see which could be the first to break out of my chest. I checked the clock. It was well past midnight.

I lay awake for hours after that, staring at the ceiling. I couldn't get Barry Bagsley out of my mind. I thought about my life since I had met him. I relived over and over every insult, every push and shove, every taunt, every sneer, every arrogant laugh, every spiteful trick, every put-down and every lost battle.

It was quite a while before I eventually got back to sleep that night. By the time I did, my mind was made up. This had all gone on too long. Barry Bagsley was finally going to pay for everything he had done.

Not only that, but I had worked out exactly how and when I was going to deliver the bill.

Part 5

Delight is to him – a far, far upward, and
inward delight – who against the proud gods
and commodores of this earth, ever stands
forth his own inexorable self.

HERMAN MELVILLE, *Moby Dick*

45.
THE TRADITIONAL END-OF-YEAR ASSEMBLY/MASS/ PRIZE-GIVING/ SPEECH NIGHT/ EXTRAVAGANZA THINGY

he night of the traditional end-of-year assembly/
mass/prize-giving/speech night/extravaganza thingy
was hot and humid. This didn't surprise me at all,
because the night of the traditional end-of-year assembly/
mass/prize-giving/speech night/ extravaganza thingy

was always hot and humid. Apparently it was some kind of meteorological law.

Mum dropped me off at the school gates. Normally the end-of-year do was a family affair, but Mum had a charity dinner she couldn't miss and Dad was babysitting Prue, who was running a temperature. I told her it was probably brain fever, from overuse. Prue said if that was the case, it was a condition to which I was permanently immune. Never tangle with a near-genius – even a sick one.

Anyway, I made the long trek from the entrance to the school gym and followed the stream of people inside. At the front of the rapidly filling hall was a large stage draped in house banners and school colours and loaded down with huge clumps of flowers. Throughout the hall, hundreds of programmes fluttered under flushed faces like nervous moths about to take flight. There was only 15 minutes to go before the evening kicked off.

Miss Tarango, who was in charge of the readers, was standing to the right of the stage searching the crowd. I stepped back behind a large banner at the side of the hall. I really should have reported in by now. But I had my own searching to do. I was on the lookout for a too-familiar sprout of blonde hair and a defiant swagger.

It wasn't long before I found what I'd been looking for. Barry Bagsley entered the gym with a steady flow of latecomers and stopped for a moment just inside the door to speak with Danny Wallace. A lot of people were still milling around chatting and trying to find seats. I drifted towards the back of the gym and waited. When Danny Wallace finally moved away, I slipped my hand into my pocket and headed in Barry Bagsley's direction. I felt like a hired assassin. By the time Barry Bagsley turned my way I was standing right beside him.

"Well, if it isn't Manure, the creature from Le Sewer. What's your problem?"

"I just came to tell you that you were wrong," I said as calmly as I could.

"Wrong? What are you crapping on about now?"

"The other day – something you said – you were wrong."

"And what was that?" Barry Bagsley said with a curled lip.

"Well, you said that I didn't have a prayer. But you're wrong. I have got a prayer. Here," I said, pulling a folded piece of paper from my pocket and handing it to him. "I even made a copy for you."

"What is this shit...?"

But I didn't wait around to hear any more. I left Barry Bagsley with his face screwed up in a sneer and headed towards Miss Tarango, who was now waving at me a little frantically.

I don't remember much at all about what happened while Prindabel, Razza, Bill and I waited for the signal from Miss Tarango to move on to the stage. I'm sure there were the usual welcoming speeches and ceremonies, but all I had on my mind was what I was about to do. I spent most of the time staring at my reading. It wasn't the one that Mr Barker had helped me write. This was one I had composed all by myself. It was the one that I had just handed to Barry Bagsley, and it was the same one I was about to read to the entire school. I let my eyes drift over the words. They seemed so simple, so harmless – just marks on a page. I read them to myself for the hundredth time.

Let us pray that Barry Bagsley can learn to let other people be themselves instead of bullying them and putting them down all the time.

I felt a hand on my shoulder. It was Miss Tarango's.
Soon we were climbing up the steps to the rostrum and
lining up behind the big lectern.

I looked around the packed gym. Three large banks
of chairs stretched to the back wall – a wide middle
section and two narrower sections at the sides. It didn't
take long to find Barry Bagsley. He was sitting about
halfway back, almost dead centre. He didn't look happy.
In fact it was one of those occasions when the expression
'bristling with anger' was right on the money. His eyes
had turned into dark slits and his mouth was a quivering
snarl. I'm sure it was only my imagination, but he looked
like he was growling. If he'd been a dog the Council
would have declared him dangerous and had him put
down on the spot.

The amazing thing was, even though I knew that
Barry Bagsley wanted to rip me limb from limb, I didn't
care. I was going to get my revenge and there was no
way he could stop me. After all, what could he do? Stand
up in front of everyone and tell me to shut up? Climb
up on the stage and crash-tackle me? Take me out with
a burst of machine gun fire? No, he was powerless. I had
Barry Bagsley right where I wanted him.

Prindabel was the first to step up and deliver his petition. I didn't hear a word he said. My eyes were locked on Barry Bagsley. He was shaking his head slightly and glaring at me while his lips seemed to be forming words. I didn't need an interpreter. I got the message loud and clear. It went something along the lines of *Don't do it, Manure. Don't even think about it, or I'll tear your head off and insert it up your backside.*

Prindabel stepped down from the lectern and Razza took his place. I shuffled a couple of steps closer.

Barry Bagsley continued to glower at me while Razza read his petition, but when he finished, the first crack appeared. Barry Bagsley broke eye contact with me, shot a quick glance to his left and right and shifted uncomfortably in his seat.

Bill Kingsley moved slowly in behind the microphone.

I studied Barry Bagsley closely. Something was happening. Although he was trying to maintain a fierce glare, he couldn't do it. His eyes kept darting to the sides, and once he twisted right around to take a fleeting look at the back of the hall. When he locked eyes with me again, his expression contorted and swirled through a range of emotions. And somewhere among all the arrogance, anger, defiance and threat, there were brief but unmistakable flashes of panic.

Bill finished his reading.

I moved forward and stepped up on to the small platform at the base of the lectern. The microphone hovered near my mouth. Barry Bagsley was squirming in his seat. His face looked like dough. He was still shaking his head at me, but there was no threat in it any more.

Then I saw a hand reach across and settle gently on his knee. It came from the lady beside him. I hadn't really noticed her before. She turned towards Barry Bagsley and leaned in with a concerned smile. I could tell she was asking if he was all right. It had to be Mrs Bagsley, but it didn't seem possible. It was hard enough imagining Barry Bagsley with a mother at all (surely he was thrown together in some dingy rat-infested laboratory) let alone one who looked... well... nice. I watched as she turned back and whispered something to the man on her right. Mr Bagsley? Why wasn't he dressed in flip-flops and football shorts, belching and drunkenly abusing the people around him? What was he doing in a suit and tie, smiling at his wife and squeezing her hand? I didn't have time to work this out. I had a job to do and I wasn't going to let anything distract me.

I pulled the microphone lower and leaned forward. "Let us pray."

My voice filled the hall. It felt like it was coming from someone else, from somewhere outside my body. For the first time in my life I was standing in front of an audience and I didn't feel nervous. I looked down at Barry Bagsley. He had pushed himself back in his seat, like he was feeling the thrust from a rocket launch. His head was still shaking from side to side, but so slightly that only I would have noticed. His lips were still forming words, but the only ones I recognised now were, 'no', 'don't' and 'please'. I looked into his eyes. The arrogance had gone. I saw nothing but fear and desperation. They were the eyes of someone who knew there was no escape.

"Let us pray that Barry..."

I spoke slowly and clearly, and when I said his name, Barry Bagsley slumped in his seat like a boxer who knows he won't survive the next round. His eyes had changed again. Now they were dull, empty and defeated.

It was a look that was familiar to me. I had seen it before, many times. I had seen it on Kelly Faulkner's brother's face and I had seen it on Bill Kingsley's. It was a look that I had also worn.

An uneasy silence crept around the gymnasium. Everyone was waiting for me to speak. I looked one last time at Barry Bagsley. I had been dreaming about this moment every day for the last week. Now it had arrived. I was about to get my revenge.

I started my petition again. I wanted to do this properly.

"Let us pray…"

I had the harpoon in my hand.

"… that Barry…"

I drew it back and steadied myself.

"… that Barry…"

All I had to do was unleash it.

"… that… barriers which separate us and keep us apart can be overcome and that we can learn to get along with each other."

46.
HOT SPACE CHICKS GET NAKED

Yeah, I know what I said. That I was going to make Barry Bagsley pay. That nothing was going to stop me. So what happened? Why didn't I go through with it? Well, I guess Barry Bagsley's mother had a lot to do with it.

You see, even as I had Barry Bagsley in my sights and I was imagining my final victory, I couldn't stop thinking about Mrs Bagsley and how embarrassed and hurt and sad she was going to be because of me. She just didn't deserve it – neither did her husband. And neither did Miss Tarango, who was so proud of our debating team and who I would be letting down, nor did Brother Jerome, who would have the school's big night ruined, nor did Mr Barker, who would be left with another mess to sort out. And they weren't the only ones. There were all the families and friends who had come along and all the people who had worked so hard on the decorations and the flowers and the music to make the evening a success – did they deserve to have their night spoilt?

And what about my own family? How would they feel when they found out what I had done?

But there was another reason why I couldn't go through with it. It was that look on Barry Bagsley's face, the one that I had put there, the one that reminded me of Kelly Faulkner's little brother, of Bill Kingsley and of myself. I didn't want to be the kind of person that made people look like that. No matter who they were. I can't really explain how I was feeling when I returned to my seat and waited for the evening to come to an end. I knew I had made the right decision and I was glad that it was all over, but nothing I had done would help Bill Kingsley. As much as I tried to convince myself that the holidays might bring him some relief, I knew they would soon pass like the eye of the storm and then Cyclone Barry would return to wreak havoc again. I was still trying to work things out in my mind when I heard Brother Jerome wishing everyone a safe trip home, and then the gym disintegrated into a rumbling mass of noise and movement.

I desperately needed some fresh air to clear my head.

"Ishmael, are you feeling all right? You had me a little worried up there tonight."

It was Miss Tarango.

"Yeah, what was that all about? Were you having a brain explosion? No, wait on, that's a bit optimistic – maybe *half* a brain explosion?"

I'll let you guess who that was.

"I'm fine. It was nothing. I was just… using pauses for dramatic effect – like you told us to, Miss."

"Is that right?" Miss Tarango said suspiciously. "Well, you might need to work on that a bit more. Anyway, well done all of you – and not just for tonight. Now off you go and have a well-earned break and I'll see you back, bigger and better, next year. "

"Yeah, see ya, Miss. You have a good holiday too. Try not to get too lonely without us."

Miss Tarango clasped her hands on her chest,

fluttered her eyelids and sighed. "Oh Orazio, how will I ever cope? It will be just devastating to have to lie on the beach day after day without even a single English essay to keep me company. But you know me. I'm a trouper. I'll struggle through... somehow."

That made us laugh. It also made us imagine Miss Tarango lying on a beach.

"We could always whip up some practice essays for you to take with you?" Razza suggested.

"Don't even think about it," Miss Tarango said as she unleashed her dimples at each of us, "not if you value your lives. Ciao, boys!"

We watched as she threaded her way through the crowd. Some teachers made school worth coming back to.

"Well, I'm off," Ignatius Prindabel announced bluntly. "It's been... interesting. Gentlemen," he said, nodding at the three of us before departing.

"I hate it when Prindabel gets all soppy," Razza said, pretending to wipe a tear from his eye before turning his attention to the moping form beside him. "Well, Bilbo, tell me, what have you got planned for the holidays? Putting the finishing touches to the time machine? Darning up the holes in your Spidey suit?

Taking a bus trip over to the Dark Side? Changing the bulb in your light sabre?"

Bill shook his head gloomily. "Nothing much," he said without emotion, "just hanging around at home... prob'ly go to the cinema or something."

I searched Bill's face. The hero of the debating finals was nowhere to be seen. There had to be some way to bring him back again. But how?

As usual, it was Razza who broke my train of thought.

"Cinema? What're you seeing?"

Bill shrugged his shoulders. "*Star Warrior's Quest – The Ultimate Evil* I guess. I have to see that."

"Yeah, all right! *The Ultimate Seagull*. Is that out already? Sweet! Man, that'd be wicked. I'm there. So when are we going, Billy Boy?"

I looked at Razza in disbelief.

"It's *Ultimate Evil*, not *Seagull*," Bill Kingsley said, screwing up his face.

"Yeah, right, *Evil*. That's what I said, *Star Worrier's Guest – The Ultimate Evil*."

"That's *Star Warrior's Quest*."

"Yeah, yeah, whatever. So when are we going?"

"I... I'm not sure... *I* was thinking of going next

week probably... maybe Tuesday."

"Great. Tuesday's good for me. What about you, Ishmael? Are you in or what?"

"Well, yeah... okay... sure... I mean, that's if it's all right with Bill."

"All right? Why wouldn't it be all right? What's the problem? You don't mind us tagging along, do you, Billy?"

A flicker of life blinked into Bill Kingsley's confused eyes. "No... I... that'd be fine... yeah, good... great."

"It's a done deal then. Oh man, *Star Warrior's Quest*! I dig that Star Warrior dude."

Finally Bill Kingsley creased his brow and asked the question that had also been bouncing around in my head. "But I thought you hated space stuff?"

Somehow Razza managed to look stunned and hurt at the same time. "Where *do* you get these crazy ideas from, Billy Boy? You know you've really got to stop performing those cranial probes on yourself. What are you on about? Me? Hate? Man, I've been hanging out to see *Star Warrior's Quest – The Ultimate Evil*. I'm a *Star Warrior's Quest* freak. It rocks. It's fully sick, man. I'm a regular Questie – a certified Quest-head. I'm a space *nut*. I'm telling you, my brain is filled with nothing *but* space!"

"So which one's your favourite, then?" Bill asked suspiciously.

Razza looked perplexed. "My favourite what?"

"Favourite *Star Warrior's Quest* film. Mine's *Star Warrior's Quest – Assassins of the King*, but a lot of people reckon *Star Warrior's Quest – The Scroll of Sorrow* is better."

Razza nodded his head thoughtfully and bit his lip. Then he tapped his fingertips together before giving his considered response. "Actually, the one I prefer is *Star Warrior's Quest – Hot Space Chicks Get Naked*. You may not be familiar with it. It only enjoyed a limited release, but it does have a strong cult following, and while I admit that the plot and dialogue leave a *little* to be desired, I feel that the cinematography – particularly the use of close-up – is breathtaking."

Bill Kingsley stood with his mouth open. Finally he recovered sufficiently to respond. "Don't tell me you haven't seen the first two parts of the *Star Warrior's Quest* trilogy?"

"All right, I won't tell you, but you'll probably work it out for yourself when I have to ask you a million questions during the film. Do you think it could lessen my viewing experience?"

Bill shook his head, overwhelmed by Razza's ignorance. "*The Ultimate Evil* is the *final* part. You won't have a clue what's going on. You won't know anything about Zabattaan and the lost Orb of Morglard Blarkon. You won't even know why Kraakon has to get the last Delfini Sun Sword in order to stop the Tempest of Vermatton from being unleashed. And you'll have no idea about the Mucallion Death Crystal or the Oath of Enlightenment or the Scales of the Seventh Serpent."

Razza tilted his head towards me and spoke from the corner of his mouth. "What language is he using now?"

"Look, it's pointless seeing the last *Star Warrior's Quest* if you haven't seen the first two."

"And I suppose you guys have both seen them?"

Bill and I nodded together. "I've seen them heaps of times. I've got the special edition DVD box sets at home – with three hours of extra features."

Suddenly Razza's eyes lit up and he slapped his forehead. "Well, that's it! Bilbo, you're a genius. Why didn't I think of it?" he said, grinning madly at our uncomprehending faces. "It's obvious – *Star Warrior's Quest* movie marathon this weekend – at the Hobbit's house! Whatta you say, Billy Boy? Are you ready to fire up the old DVD player?"

"Well… yeah… yeah, sure… okay… why not?"

"Woohoo! You da bomb, Billy! You – da – Bomb!"

"Bill, you sure that's okay? Maybe you've got other plans or something. Razza can always rent the movies out himself, you know."

"No, it's fine… I'll have to check with Mum… but that's no problem… really… it'll be fine… if you guys want to come over… it'll be great."

"Sure it'll be great. Come on, Billy Boy," Razza said, throwing his arm around Bill Kingsley's broad shoulders. "We have to plan this thing to within a millimetre of its life. Ishmael, we'll give you a ring when we've got all the details sorted out. Geez, this is gonna be a big operation – two films plus three hours of special effects. We could be talking sleepover here, B.K."

Bill Kingsley shook his head as he let himself be swept away in the avalanche of Razza's enthusiasm. I wasn't worried, though. He'd survive. The smile on his face told me so.

"Now, we'll need food and lots of it. You have to watch your diet, Big Guy, so I'll be in charge of catering.

We've got to make sure we cover the three basic food groups – pizzas, chips and ice cream. No whingeing. It's for your own good."

"You da boss," Bill Kingsley said.

Razza staggered back in amazement. "You got that right, big fella! Now let's go find your mum and get the ball rolling. Catch you later, Ishmael."

"Yeah, see ya guys… and Razz… don't get *too* carried away, okay?"

"Carried away? Moi?"

Razza wheeled Bill Kingsley around. The last thing I heard him say as they headed off was, "Now, Billy Boy… about the beer and strippers…"

I heard a strange noise come from deep within Bill Kingsley. It took me a moment to realise that he was laughing.

Razza looked back at me, flashed that deadly smile and gave me the thumbs up.

They were right all along. The Razzman really did work in mysterious ways.

47.
HANNIBAL LECTER'S MUM

As I watched Razza and Bill Kingsley disappear into the crowd, I knew nothing would ever wipe the smile off my face.

"S'pose you thought that was funny."

I turned around. The smile was wiped off my face.

"I wasn't trying to be funny."

The eyes that met mine sizzled with anger. They belonged to Barry Bagsley. "I knew you wouldn't have the guts to go through with it," he said, spitting the words at me.

I didn't bother arguing with him. I had seen his face from the stage. We both knew the truth.

"I just want you to lay off Bill Kingsley, that's all."

"If I were you, I'd be more worried about myself. Maybe you got away with it for tonight, but there won't be anywhere to hide next year."

He was right. But it didn't matter. I'd had enough of trying to make myself small. I didn't want to be the invisible boy any more. "I won't be hiding," I told him.

We stood facing each other in an awful silence. I wouldn't have been surprised to see a tumbleweed roll between us.

"Barry – there you are! I've lost your father completely. He's vanished off the face of the earth. Probably melted somewhere in that suit of his. Oh… I'm sorry – didn't see you there," Mrs Bagsley said, turning towards me. "Hello."

It was like coming face to face with Hannibal Lecter's mum.

"Hi."

But how did Hannibal end up with a mother like that? She was too young, too… good-looking… too bright and bubbly. When she smiled her face lit up like one of those people on an info-commercial. At any minute I expected her to try to sell me some revolutionary exercise machine to help tighten my non-existent abs.

"Barry, where are your manners? Aren't you going to introduce me to your friend?"

Luckily Mrs Bagsley was looking at me, so she didn't see her son grimace like he'd been hit in the face with a steel frying pan.

"He's not..."

Mrs Bagsley turned her dazzling smile on her son.

"Um... this is... he's... Ishmael." Barry Bagsley said my name like he'd been forced to swallow poison.

"Ishmael? What a lovely name. Quite unusual."

I don't know if it was because his mother was so friendly or whether it was because of the look of horror that was deepening on Barry Bagsley's face, but for once I decided not to run away from my name.

"It's from *Moby Dick* – the novel. The narrator's called Ishmael. I was named after him. It's a long story."

"How *in*teresting," Mrs Bagsley gushed, before something caught her eye. "Barry, look, there's your father – near the back. You're going to have to rescue him from Mrs Armbruster before she chews both his ears off. I'll meet you both at the back door – no need for all of us to suffer," she said with a wink. "Ishmael, it was lovely to meet you. I don't get the chance to talk with many of Barry's friends – most of them don't seem to be that chatty. Perhaps you could arrange with Barry to come over sometime during the holidays. You'd be very welcome."

Barry Bagsley looked like he was about to bring up his lower intestine. I thought I'd give him a hand.

"Sounds great."

"Well, you two sort it out. But Barry, be quick. I don't think your father can last much longer."

"Goodbye, Ishmael."

"'Bye, Mrs Bagsley."

Barry Bagsley waited until his mother was out of sight before pointing his finger at me and narrowing his eyes. He seemed to be struggling to find words that could match the emotions raging inside him.

"Next year," he said somehow making those two simple words sound like a bomb threat.

"I'll be there," I said, and for the first time in ages, I knew it would be true.

48.
GREAT: ADJECTIVE – LARGE, ENORMOUS, MASSIVE; UNUSUAL OR EXTREME – AS IN GREAT JOY

Now I definitely needed that fresh air.

"Mr Leseur – a word, if you would."

There was no mistaking that voice. "Mr Barker?" I said, desperately trying to think what crime I might have unknowingly committed.

"I have just been speaking with Brother Jerome."

This didn't sound good at all.

"Apparently we've had a telephone call from James Scobie's father, and…"

"Is James all right?" I broke in before I could stop myself.

Mr Barker raised his eyebrows before continuing. "Well, as I was about to say, it seems that the *personal* and *family* matters they were concerned about were found, on closer examination, not to be concerns at all."

"Great… that's great… that's… great!" (Great: adjective – large, enormous, massive; unusual or extreme – as in great joy; also *colloquial*: very good or fine, exceptional, fantastic, sensational, terrific.)

"I see that all that debating has turned you into quite an orator, Mr Leseur."

"Then James is coming back to school next year?"

"Yes, we shall have the unique pleasure of Mr Scobie's company right from the very first day."

"Great!"

"Well, as riveting as your sparkling repartee is," Mr Barker said as he glared towards the back of the hall, where Doug Savage and Danny Wallace were involved in some sort of tag-team wrestling match with two other boys, "I'm afraid I must leave you. There are some heads I have to bang together."

"Thanks for letting me know about James, Mr Barker. See you next year. I think you have us for Citizenship again then."

"Great," Mr Barker mumbled as he strode off.

As I turned and headed towards the exit, not even a platoon of Barry Bagsleys armed with loaded bazookas could have wiped the smile off my face.

49.
THE MOST
IMPORTANT BIT

It was time to make the long journey to the front gates, where Dad had arranged to pick me up. I took one last look at the remaining clumps of people scattered about the hall. There were no familiar faces. Fresh air, here I come!

I would have made it too, if I hadn't been involved in a head-on collision with someone who chose that precise moment to rush back into the gym.

"Ishmael! Thank god you're still here."

Ignatius Prindabel looked decidedly flustered.

"I've been carrying this around all night and then I almost forgot it. My life would have been hell. Here," he said, puffing out a breath and pushing a small envelope at me. My name was printed on the front in green pen.

"What's this?"

"Don't know. Don't care. Someone from my stupid sister's school gave it to my stupid sister to give to me to give to you. I just gave it to you. My work here is done. So long."

"Yeah, but... okay, see ya, Ignatius... and thanks for..."

But he had already vanished into the night. I moved to a quiet spot behind some stacked up chairs. I turned the envelope over in my hand before opening it and pulling out the single sheet of yellow paper that was inside. It had a border of tiny butterflies and it was filled with neat handwriting. I glanced down to the bottom of the page searching for a name.

My heart stopped.

I shot back to the start and began to read.

Dear Ishmael,

If you are reading this then I guess that Cynthia Prindabel got her brother to pass it on to you.

If you're not reading it then – well – okay, let's just assume you are reading it!

I guess you're wondering what this is all about.

Well, let me explain. My friend Sally Nofke turns fifteen next month and she's invited me to her party. She wants it to be a mixed party but the trouble is she's short on boys. That's where you come in! I told her about how you helped Marty and how you were a sidekick to a superhero and everything and she was pretty impressed. Sally said it would be great if you could come to her party and maybe bring the Razzman along too. (That's if he's not too busy fighting crime and stuff.)

I know that is a long way off but by the time you get this note I will be already holidaying with my folks in New Zealand and I won't be back until the weekend before school starts next year. I thought I might as well give you some time to think about it and then if you're interested you can ring me and I can give you all the details.

Hope you and your friend can come along.

Best wishes

Kelly Faulkner

PS D'oh! Nearly forgot the most important bit –
   my phone number is 4060 8699 so...
   call me Ishmael!

50.
THE MOTHER OF ALL WILD, BARBARIC YAWPS

Nothing could stop me now. I bolted from the gym and ran straight through the school grounds and across the main oval where Peter Chung had taken on the Magnon. And I kept running until my chest was burning and my legs felt like lumps of wood and I didn't stop until I found myself in the middle of The Fields where Kelly Faulkner's little brother had been bullied. Then I sank to my knees and rolled back on to the cool grass, gasping for air.

When my chest stopped heaving, I pulled out Kelly Faulkner's letter and read it through in the strong moonlight. Once again the familiar last line exploded from the page and jolted my heart. But I got it wrong. I didn't scream like I said I would. Instead I closed my eyes, threw back my head and let out the mother of all wild, barbaric yawps, and for the first time in ages, I felt alive and I felt whole again.

But do you want to know the really weird thing? Well, I'll tell you. The really weird thing was that as I lay there with only the raspy sound of my breathing filling my ears and with the spongy grass of St Daniel's playing fields buoying me up, I could have sworn that I was floating and bobbing on the surface of a vast green ocean. Remind you of anyone?

Go on – call me Ishmael if you like.

After all, as the Big Z would say, I'm da man!

ACKNOWLEDGEMENTS

Thanks above all to my wife Adriana, for continuing to find me 'tolerable', and for writing all the very best bits of my life; also to my daughter Meg, for not letting on yet that she's far more talented than her father.

Extra special thanks this time around to my son Joe, for taking time out from being the next Spielberg to cast his expert eye over the manuscript and for bringing 'Ringo' to life.

My immense gratitude, as always, goes to the good folk at Omnibus Books and Scholastic Australia, especially the dynamic duo of Dyan Blacklock and Celia Jellett, who continue to make it possible for my dreams to come true.

Heartfelt thanks also to family, friends, colleagues, acquaintances and strangers who have said such lovely things about the first book and encouraged me to keep writing.

Finally, thank you to Marist College, Ashgrove and schools like it that celebrate the worth of the individual and challenge their students to 'act courageously'.

THE AUTHOR

When quizzed about his own memories of school, author Michael Gerard Bauer recollects three things clearly:

1. His ambition was to become a Samurai warrior.
2. Standing in front of his fellow students was as daunting a prospect for him as it is for his central character, Ishmael.
3. He never thought about writing.

Fortunately for his readers, soon after graduating from the University of Queensland, Michael quickly traded in his dreams of martial arts expertise, became a teacher and began to write.

Michael has since discovered that he is, after all, rather good at writing and has received a raft of awards for *Don't Call Me Ishmael*, including the 2008 South Australian Festival Award for Literature, the 2007 Children's Peace Prize. In 2007 he was also shortlisted for the CBCA Award for Older Readers and the White Ravens festival at the Bologna Book Fair.

Michael now lives in the beautiful Brisbane suburb of Ashgrove with his family. *Don't Call Me Ishmael* is his first book to be published in the UK.

Another Templar book you might enjoy...

Ishmael and the Return of the Dugongs

MICHAEL GERARD BAUER

Ishmael and his friends are back at St Daniel's for another year of misadventure, with Ishmael's best mate Razz determined to set him up with the girl of his dreams, Kelly.

Unfortunately the path of true love never did run smooth, and before Ishmael can win Kelly's heart, he has to overcome a mortifying pool incident, a painful knockout, and getting caught red-handed with her diary.

The only solution to Ishmael's situation lies with his Dad's rock band – but can the Dugongs set everything right?

May 2012   Paperback   £6.99

ISBN 978-1-84877-712-5